D0984413

*The Housewife and the Assassin*

SUSAN TROTT. . . . .

# The Housewife

# and the Assassin

. . . . . St. Martin's Press, New York

Copyright 1979 by Susan Trott
All rights reserved. For information, write:
St. Martin's Press
175 Fifth Avenue
New York, N.Y. 10010
Manufactured in the United States of America
Library of Congress Catalog Card Number: 78-69745

**Library of Congress Cataloging in Publication Data**

Trott, Susan.
   The housewife and the assassin.

   I. Title.
PZ4.T8577Ho   [PS3570.R594]   813'.5'4   78-69745
ISBN 0-312-39346-6

To George Leonard, Claudia Shenefield, Chuck Weesner, Emery Mitchell, Millicent Tomkins— for the hundreds of miles we ran, the good talks, and the love.

# . . . . . *Prologue*

A transcontinental telephone conversation:

"Do you know anything about this woman Augusta Gray, who was shot down in San Francisco awhile back under such odd circumstances? I smelled a good story there, but I haven't been able to reach you."

"Because I've been writing it. In the guise of a novel, of course. Now I only have to check out a few things and I'll be sending it on to you: the whole story regarding Augusta Gray and her jogging book."

*The Housewife and the Assassin*

# PART ONE

# 1

## . . . . . *The International Jogging Idea*

AUGUSTA got the idea while standing among the flamboyant fresh fruits at the Mill Valley Market, not a usual place for ideas with her, since the beautiful produce—especially the lemons and eggplants—inclined to make her feel giddy, mildly elated, so that she tended to bask in all this beauty with the look of one who is being massaged.

A jogging book! An international jogging book for businessmen—and women—for traveling business persons, and ne'er-do-wells too. A handy guide for the traveler-who-runs to find at a glance the likeliest place to jog in each of the major cities of the world.

It wasn't a new idea to her. She had sometimes thrown it out to jogging friends who were international businessmen but who, in a foreign city, didn't have time to find out the best place to run, where the traffic conditions would be acceptable and where the embarrassment quotient would be low. But now, now among the glowing foods, the idea struck her in such a way that she knew she would do it, could do it, that it was a possible plan. She would begin today.

In her cart she placed a head of ruffled red lettuce, spinach, radishes, and green onions and pushed along to the canned seafoods. A woman in her late thirties was Augusta: five six, slim, red hair austerely arranged, delicate features, large round brown eyes presently out of focus from thinking about her idea, a light wandering step. She wore nice suburban clothes along with an air of folly that suggested something ethereal and unsubstantial about her composition.

Illustrated with maps, of course. There must be maps. Routes clearly described. Jogging courses in all the great capitals of the world. It will depend a great deal on Duke, for he is the great traveler, and it is he who understands cities and maps and transportation. I could not do it without Duke.

And how he will enjoy it! It will take some large amount of time to do—he will have to quit his job, but he works so very hard that quitting will be nice for him. What a happy time we will have traveling about the world together doing this book.

Even thinking to herself, Augusta found that she could not sustain the future tense and slipped into the conditional.

I know Duke would like it. Wouldn't he? He would become a well and happy man. We would become partners and boon companions in this venture, instead of husband and wife. In fact, the book could be more than just a simple handbook and guide. INTERNATIONAL JOGGING: *A Marital and Physical Odyssey in Which a Young Fit Wife and Old Unfit Husband Go Jogging Together in the Great Capitals of the World.* Duke would stop smoking, lose weight, become lean as a whippet. The book could contain before-and-after pictures!

Augusta was now in front of the canned fishes, looking abstracted. Something else . . . yes, it should also be a mystical odyssey, to satisfy my California readers.

"Chopped clams for the clam sauce," said her daughter Lee, who, having finished a conversation with a friend among the frozen foods, now joined her mother.

Augusta turned to her lovely youngest, whose body and carriage already had the supernatural look of the ballerina although she was only twelve. "Oh, yes, run to the vegetables, then, and get a bouquet of parsley. I forgot it."

The girls. What about the girls? Could they come too? No, not practical. It would complicate the odyssey hopelessly.

But she had never left her girls. In her childbearing years she had been overwhelmingly impressed by Freud's declaration that the first year was the *most* important—so she had never given either child over to anyone else's care, positively avoiding any unknown trauma, nursing them both a full twelve months to cleave them close, to shelter them. Then, she considered, mightn't the next nine years be awfully important too? Not enough to keep on nursing, surely, but important enough to stay nearby?

At this time Neill was teacher: freedom without permissiveness; teaching through love and respect, not fear. She never struck them, although she had vented her rage sometimes in vigorous shakings and more than once had to control the impulse towards a Dickensian box on the ear.

It had all worked out just fine. They were loving, happy, confident. They were good kids. Now they were twelve and sixteen, and it was time to let them go. Enter the third teacher, Wild Animal Mother, who readied her offspring for life, taught them all she knew that was useful, and pushed them out on their own, gently released them, relinquished them to the predestined environment: jungle, savannah, suburb, or urb.

Freud, Neill, and Wild Animal had advised her well in the raising of her two girls. They would be all right without her while she created this book and transformed her marriage.

If she could just push herself out of the nest, that is. For the last year, Augusta had been unable to go anywhere alone. Even on a simple shopping expedition to the town square, she needed to take Duke, a daughter, or a friend. She suffered, she supposed, from agoraphobia—fear of the marketplace.

The interesting, really amazing thing was that no one,

not even her family, knew this. She had contrived to hide this incapacitating disease, or unease, from everyone.

Now Augusta crossed the town square to her car, keeping her eye on Lee to assure herself she was not alone, which seemed miraculously to hold the anxiety-inducing vertigo at bay. Her little wisp of a daughter did not know that she was sustaining her mother in this way or realize how grateful Augusta was for her presence.

They and an obliging bag boy bundled the marketing into the car that Augusta hated. It was a 1959 Mercedes 220 SL black four-door sedan. Because of her husband's parsimony, she had never had a car that ran well or that she felt safe in. "Tighter than a cow's ass in the fly season," she mumbled whenever she thought of this. It was a phrase she'd found in a Western and kept to describe Duke, under her breath, when they had money dealings together. It was one of her most treasured quotations.

This car, which he had bought from a friend and was very proud of, took the cake. She didn't mind that it needed bodywork. That, if anything, redeemed it, kept it from being the ostentatious car which, despite its age, or because of it, it couldn't help being by virtue of its Mercedesness and big-black-handsomeness of design. The interior was, cosmetically, a disaster area. Duke talked about restoring it, but he never would. Why not admit it and say, as Count Dracula did when asked if he would restore the crumbling old castle he had bought in England, "No. I am going to keep it *exactly* like it is."

The engine was powerful and the car was substantial, so that was a comfort—but the bald front tires were not a comfort, nor was the shimmy the car developed when it hit fifty, nor did she like the smoke it belched when she ignited the engine. In addition, it was hard to maneuver, impossible to parallel park because of its size and stiffness. One of the kids had to help her turn the steering wheel to execute any really tight turn.

All this was tolerable. The real reason for her hatred was that it smacked to her of Hitler and SS troops, no matter that she wasn't a Jew. One needen't be a Jew to not want a big black German car. Anyhow, she wished she was a Jew—she was not sure why. She did not mind being a Wasp. The first twenty years of one's life there wasn't much choice, and she knew she'd been extremely lucky. Born into a socially registered Boston family, she had been given the best: private education, summer home on the North Shore, a European tour at eighteen with headquarters at her parents' villa in Spain, a debut at the Boston Cotillion, membership in the Junior League, acceptance at an Ivy League college.

But at twenty she surprised herself, and everyone else, due to a quote from Whistler (ever since she could first read, Augusta had secured quotes to guide her): "I was born in Lawrence, Massachusetts, but I do not choose to have been born in Lawrence, Massachusetts."

This made a great impression on her. As the nearest hospital to her family's country home in Andover was in Lawrence, she too had been born there—and Lawrence is a horrible town. She understood a world of choice was open to her, going back to her birth and on to her death. She did not need to tread a predictable path. She could choose to change anything, even her birthplace.

She thought, I too do not choose to have been born in Lawrence, and what's more, I do not choose to be a Boston debutante at an Ivy League college. Ha-ha! So she left it all, went west in a gradual fashion, camping out, seeing America. On the Coast she reencountered Duke Gray, whom she had originally met vagabonding through Spain, and she married him. She believed in his nomadic spirit even though he'd gone to Princeton—one of the great backers of predictable path treading—where a man tends to be programmed into the eventual role of high-powered executive. Duke, unbeknownst to Augusta, was in the second stage of this program, having just decided to put the cap on his rambles (wild oats all sown) and marry, have children, get rich.

Augusta, then, having discovered Choice, made a bad one. All unknowing, she rebelled herself into a contract with one who was finished rebelling and who hungered for his return to the program.

To finish with the subject of cars, when Augusta was eighteen she had seen and been enticed by a graceful and easy sports car called Austin Healey. It was a car to take on long stretches of country roads, up and down mountains, along the shores of seas. She thought that if she could ever have a car of her own, the Healey would be the only one to have.

They were no longer produced, but recently she had seen one for sale at Fantasy Junction. Threading her way through parked Rollses, Bentleys, and rumble-seated early Americana, she inquired and was amazed to discover the reasonable price of three thousand dollars, cheaper than the cheapest new American car. If she got a thousand for the hated Mercedes, then the Healey would only cost her two! There were drawbacks. It was not a family-size car. Duke probably wouldn't sell the Mercedes, which could well be *his* fantasy car. Also, as far as anyone knew, Augusta did not have two thousand dollars.

Still, she entertained the notion, was tempted to think of herself for once. Why not indulge myself, she thought, before I am too old? Why not be carefree and impractical for a change, seize this pleasure?

She sneaked in for a test drive. It grieved her that she had become a sneak during the years of her marriage to Duke, but it eventually became the only way she could operate. So she stole in and drove it away with the top down and three kids, Lee and two friends, crammed in with her. They went wheeling all about the town with their hair flying and . . . and, alas, she did not like it. She was not happy in that car. She felt embarrassed. She felt like a show-off, a show-off trying to get attention, trying to get laid perhaps. She felt exposed and ridiculous. And old. She had got too old for this fantastical car, too old and too sneaky.

Now, marketing all stowed, Augusta and Lee wrestled the Mercedes out of the parking space and headed for the library to pick up her sixteen-year-old daughter, Val. Augusta was still thinking of her International Jogging Book.

She did not know that her life had taken a turn, had begun radically to change, that the idea born amongst the vegetables was to generate intrigue, discord, and danger in her ostensibly sheltered and pleasant life.

She could not know that something horrible would happen to her, a catastrophe. But if, when it did happen, she could look back through her life and try to pinpoint exactly when it all began, she would see it was there—there in the market when she got her idea.

Unless the "something horrible" turns out to be death, in which case any looking backwards to find the beginning of the end becomes academic. But if she survives the catastrophe, surely there is something to be learned from all that went before—as in "live and learn."

Can you die and learn?

# 2

..... *Ephraim and*
*Evalyn in Suva*

WHERE was Augusta's killer on this same day in March?
While Augusta went about her humble errands, what was
he doing, and could it have had any possible connection
with what was on the slate for him and Augusta?

It could, it did—for he had just met Evalyn. Hard to
say if it was exactly the same time, or even the same
day, as he was not only in another time zone but also
across the international date line at the Grand Pacific
Hotel in Suva, Fiji—a grand hotel on the harbor, built at
the turn of the century, surrounded by gardens, lawns,
the cricket field, rows of royal palms.

In a rattan chair beneath the slow sweep of fan in a cool, dignified, slightly seedy ambience, Ephraim was sitting by himself when he was accosted, introduced to Evalyn, and left alone with her by a mutual acquaintance who didn't know any better.

Two disparate-looking people were Ephraim Johnstone and Evalyn Ruth. Evalyn exuded charm; her hands and mouth were in constant motion. She was a short, fit-looking woman dressed in understated American good taste, except that she wore a lot of precious jewels in unusual settings. Her brown hair was short and beautifully cut to show off her fine features, just as her hands were manicured to display her rings. Her nails were like jewels in their own right.

Ephraim was dressed in understated flamboyance. He was as thrilling as one of Augusta's favorite vegetables, but one would have to look closely to appreciate what an outrage he was. Six feet five inches tall was Ephraim, and so slender that he looked even taller. Long, narrow, pale, he looked deceptively like a perfect ectomorph— but he was extremely strong. That long body was all muscle. On the somatotype scales of one to seven, he was seven parts ectomorph, two mesomorph, and one part endomorph. He considered himself the perfect body type, considered all such ecto-meso combinations supreme beings, the only ones who would endure well on into the next century. Indeed he already looked futuristic, unearthly. His large intelligent blue eyes missed nothing, although they never looked sharp or darted about. They were soft eyes that looked at nothing and saw everything, even what was behind him. His hair was red but not noticeably so in the shade of the bar. In the sun his hair lit up like the flash of a redwing blackbird stretching its wings for flight.

He was wearing a white tuxedo dress shirt with pleated front secured by moonstone studs; no tie, open collar. This superior shirt was tucked into weathered jeans. At first glance one thought (Evalyn thought) he must have been up all night after some formal function and only changed his pants for the day. But the shirt was too fresh-looking, too ironed. He obviously chose this outfit, and she was full of admiration for his audacity. But she was also disturbed, as one can be by the truly unexpected, so that her mind worried at it even as she chattered on about this and that.

Possibly, she thought, he is down to his last shirt, is insistently finicky about wearing fresh shirts each day, and found himself with only this one. But then wouldn't he simply buy a shirt? Maybe he always wears dress shirts. Oh, leave it alone, Evalyn. Screw it.

Ephraim, Evalyn soon learned, was laconic in the extreme. But she managed to extract the information that he had come to Fiji for relaxation. He had wearied of Tahiti years ago, found the Fijians to be more friendly and more beautiful, liked also the colorful and shrewd Indians who populated the islands, enjoyed the sultriness, the enforced lassitude.

Evalyn said she didn't like Tahiti anymore either.

"Really it was going downhill when Gauguin left it for the Marquesas, and now there is such bad feeling between the French and Tahitians it sheds a pall. Too bad."

She explained that she was only in Suva for the day, off a ship she was taking to the Bay of Islands, New Zealand, where she would visit with a friend for a week. Small talk. Ephraim mostly listened. He was not a talker, primarily because his work enjoined him to be a listener.

Despite his quietness, Evalyn was interested in this young man. She determined to learn more about him from the mutual acquaintance who had introduced them. If he was what she imagined—and she was fantastically intuitive and deductive—he might be useful to know. Meanwhile, it was easy for her to keep the conversational ball rolling because she was an articulate, smart, and amusing monologuist.

Ephraim thought he detected a German accent behind the American camouflage, and he was right. Her accent was imperceptible except to the keenest ear—his. Perhaps it was not accent to much as sentence construction.

Evalyn was in her forties, older than Augusta. Augusta's only personal memory of World War II was the occasional blackout and Polish DPs coming to live with her family in the large house in Andover. Evalyn remembered hunger and scrounging through garbage cans and maltreatment and always having with her a strychnine tablet—a gift from her mother, who urged her to use it when life became unendurable (then swallowed hers). Evalyn endured. She passed through the crucible and emerged a person of high-grade steel.

At seventeen she stowed away on a ship to Canada and, soon after landfall, she slipped into America. In the next twenty-eight years, applying her strength, intelligence, amorality, intuitive and deductive powers, she made herself not a cool million but fifteen cool ones, at last count. Halfway along she bought a senator to take care of her illegal entry and secured her American citizenship. She was the American success story: from garbage in cans to pheasant under glass.

She liked being rich and she liked, not power, but influence. She had a lot of it in her hometown of Sacramento and a lot of it wherever she took up residence when away: a condo in Honolulu, a suite at the Fairmont in San Francisco, a villa in Acapulco.

"Would you like to come aboard the ship for the sailing? The accommodations are extremely nice." (Nicer than the ones on the ship to Canada where she had spent five days and nights immobilized under a deck steward's bunk).

"No, thanks. I have committed myself to total inactivity. I plan many more hours in this chair."

"Your work must be wearisome," she suggested with a note of inquiry.

"I write."

"Oh?"

"I write suspense stories so complex that at the end no one is entirely sure who the murderer was or, indeed, even who, if anyone, was murdered. The critics love them. They describe them as Byzantine. Few people read them and fewer buy them."

"How fascinating. Then it must be the researching of these books that wearies you," said Evalyn acutely, "and that supports you."

"Or else I am independently wealthy."

"Good for you," Evalyn laughed. She rose to her feet, and Ephraim uncoiled himself to stand and say good-bye. "Perhaps we will meet again in San Francisco. Would you dine with me some evening?"

"I never dine."

"Should I have said eat?"

"I do eat. But alone."

"I see. Well, I guess I am terribly lucky to have had a drink with you."

"It's the sultriness of Suva. I hadn't the energy to get away."

"In short, you dislike any kind of socializing," Evalyn said more seriously.

"That's right."

"Then perhaps we shall meet again on a business proposition."

Ephraim watched Evalyn walk away and forgot her. During the time she had sat with him, about fifteen minutes, he had only given her a small portion of his attention. The rest, all of his modalities working at once, was focused on a man some few tables to the left and behind him.

Now, as he turned to reseat himself, he ascertained that the man looked replete, not to say engorged, with food and drink. He had put down a vast amount of rum and hors d'oeuvres with attendant guzzling and smacking sounds throughout—the sort of man, Ephraim thought, who had taken his high-chair mannerisms with him right into middle age. Probably the floor as well as the table would need a good scrubbing when he left. As for the grease, rum, spittle, and crumbs on his face, he probably would rub it all in, not off, and not with a napkin, but with a sleeve.

Nevertheless, the man's glittering eyes reminded Ephraim that no amount of food or drink seemed to dull this fellow's devious mind. Without seeming to look anywhere in particular, Ephraim absorbed this information instantly. He then decided to anticipate the man's departure and therefore did not regain his seat; instead, throwing down a number of Fiji dollars and taking his jean jacket over his arm, he walked nonchalantly to the lobby.

Presently, Quilp (as Ephraim called him to himself) came strolling through the lobby. Once out of doors, Ephraim was amused to see Quilp affect the Fijian style of dealing with the tropical sun by raising an umbrella. But his amusement withered as he realized that the large umbrella, which Quilp carried low over his head, would preclude a neat shot to the brain. He would have to go for the heart.

Ephraim followed his quarry in a rented car.

Quilp was the architect of a crime for which an honest boy had gone to prison. "In fact," said the boy's father, "the entire crime was concocted not for gain but so that my boy would suffer the consequences, having offended the monster by rebuffing his sexual advances." The boy, according to his father, was frail and sensitive as well as honest; he had gone to prison and there was brutalized and sodomized with a vengeance—possibly through Quilp's further intervention—and soon died. All this, although not without some small interest to Ephraim (for he always liked a little background) was a matter of indifference. The boy could have been a degenerate for all he cared, and Quilp a saint. It was just business, a business transaction between himself and the boy's father, who could afford the best.

What did interest him extremely was the umbrella complication and having to make an alteration in his modus operandi.

Fifteen minutes later, Quilp was standing on the edge of a pier and Ephraim was in the dim light of a shed surrounded by huge containers. In honor of the sailing of the S.S. *Ganymede*, the Royal Fiji Police Band had come to the pier to play. The musicians were all stunningly stalwart, handsome men. Their eyes shone; they had big, easy smiles, perfect teeth. They wore black shirts and pure white skirts wrapped smoothly around their loins and secured by a thin red belt. Quilp ingested the look of them with the same greedy, slavering pleasure he'd shown at table. The band raised their silver wind instruments—tubas, horns, trumpets, trombones—and struck up a stirring rendition of "Stars and Stripes Forever" as they marched in perfect step up and down the length of the pier.

Under cover of the shed, the music, and the general air of festival, Ephraim raised his pistol and scored a neat hit through Quilp's black heart.

Ephraim left the pistol between a container and the shed wall and joined some idlers on the pier who were beating time to the music. He was extremely pleased with himself. It was the first time he had killed someone in front of (he counted) forty-one policemen!

Quilp, meanwhile, had dropped quietly off the dock.

Soon, a cloud of crimson colored the dingy blue dock-water next to a floating umbrella. But it was some minutes before anyone noticed.

Anyone except for Evalyn, who noticed at once. Evalyn, whose appreciation of police band music was at about the same level as her admiration for the Stars and Stripes, had been standing at the ship's railing, casting about for something to amuse her, when she saw Quilp (whom she recognized from the hotel bar) being jolted off his feet and into the water. Her only reaction was a slight lifting of the eyebrows. She then looked up and down the pier and was not astonished to see her recent companion leaning against the container shed with an air of sublime insouciance.

Fascinating, she thought. Indeed, that young man will be very useful to know. How nice! She felt much as she had when, earlier that day, she'd acquired a particularly beautiful emerald from a shrewd Indian connection.

Evalyn's ship followed the curve of the earth down under while Ephraim's plane followed it upwards and over, back to Mill Valley, California, USA.

# 3

. . . . . *Augusta at Home*

AT THE library, Augusta picked up her oldest daughter, Val, who immediately rummaged through the marketing for a tangerine her sensitive fruit-detecting nose knew would be there.

"Do you want me to drop you home," Augusta asked, "or do you want to come to the track with me and Lee? I'm going to see if I can run a mile. I am going to start running so that I can write a book about it."

"Okay. I have to run around three times for the Kennedy test, so I might as well practice. As long as the track team isn't there. I'd be embarrassed if they were."

"Am I right in thinking a mile is four times around?"

"Yes."

"Dear me."

"We saw a film on jogging at school today," Val said. "There was this man who was suicidal, and he also had a bad heart. So he decided a good way to commit suicide was to run and burst his heart. So he ran, but he couldn't burst it. Every day he tried to run himself to death. Then he began to feel better. He began to feel so good that he didn't want to die anymore. And he loved running. Now he runs for the fun of it and waves to everyone and smiles and feels good and is happy. You see, a lot of people jog to lose weight, but you don't really lose all that much because your fat turns to muscle, which is just as heavy. What you do is build up your heart and keep fat from developing around it so you live longer."

"How I wish your father would exercise," Augusta said sadly. "But I am hoping to get him interested in running with this book idea. I am glad to know that about the heart. And lungs too, I imagine. It would be good for your lungs to run, Val." Val was asthmatic.

"Yeah, but it's so boring."

"It will be good for my ballet to run," said Lee.

"Ballet's not an organ of the body," said Val.

"I know that."

There were about fifteen persons running around the high school track, most of whom wore sweat suits and looked, to Augusta, shapely and fleet.

I suppose Duke and I will have to wear sweat suits, she thought nervously, knowing Duke would never submit to such an indignity.

But in cities, she thought on, if you are running and don't wear a sweat suit, people think that you are being pursued, that you are in terrible trouble. Also, the tormented expression on a jogger's face is similar to an expression of terror. Yes, we will have to wear sweat suits so as not to alarm the citizens of the great capitals of the world.

But what if I were running in a sweat suit and I really were being pursued? No one would help me. They would think I was just running.

Come on, Augusta, just get started and deal with these things as they come.

Her daughters set off around the track with nice strides. Augusta took off her sweater and began to run.

She ran around once, a quarter of a mile.

On the next lap she could not continue. She slowed, deciding to walk a little way and then try again. When she had caught her breath she began to run, but at the start of the third lap she had to walk again.

Only half a mile! And her head was throbbing, and her lungs were heaving up stuff that she was choking on while coughing, and her leg muscles felt like they were lacing themselves up the shinbones with a big bow knot at the knee.

A young man with mighty legs going like pistons passed her and said, "It gets to you, doesn't it?"

"Yes, it does," she coughed.

She began to run again, determined to go the four times around regardless—even if it meant walking the entire last lap, which it did.

She wobbled back to the car where her girls were waiting.

"Well, I *am* surprised," she said. "I thought I was in good shape what with tennis and hiking and all. You did well, Val. You did your three laps running all the way."

"Yes, but I got wheezy."

"And Lee just skimmed around all four laps easy as pie. You know . . . I thought jogging was supposed to make you feel good, but I feel just awful. Well, let's go home."

Home was in the poorer part of Mill Valley, California, USA, which is to say their house was not on the mountain or in the canyons or near the tennis club or bordering the golf course. It was on the flatland between the high school and the town square, where smallish houses stood cheek by jowl, where mostly old retired people lived, tenderly trimming little lawns and growing resplendent roses that the wealthy of the town would have eaten their hearts out to have.

As Augusta clambered from the car onto the lane where her house was, she saw that on this balmy evening (the date was March 17, St. Patrick's Day and also, according to Augusta's calendar, Evacuation Day in Boston and Suffolk County, Massachusetts, which she hoped meant that the proper Bostonians got to move their bowels) each wee yard along the lane contained a white-haired or bald person performing some lovely gesture for a plant.

She waved and smiled. Most of them were deaf, so it was not her custom to shout greetings. She looked benignly down the lane, feeling the exquisite pleasure of safe return that she always felt after accomplishing the trip to and from town, which, to her fear-burdened mind, was ever a hazardous and death-defying journey.

The girls took in the marketing, and Augusta stood just inside the gate of her picket fence under an ancient cherry tree in ultimate bloom. A soft, slight breeze stirred through the branches, releasing blossoms which wafted down like opaque flakes of gentlest snow that upon touching the grass did not melt away but remained for a day or so before losing opacity and then, like a piece of shed skin, commenced to crumple, dwindle, and dissolve.

She watched the cherry blossoms fall. She stood entranced beneath the tree and its sporadic faery flurries of petals. I can't believe I couldn't run a mile, she thought. There's one illusion smashed. I wonder how many other wrong things I think about myself?

Lots. Augusta had many illusions. She was so used to hiding things from Duke that she hid them from herself, too. One illusion was that she had a good marriage and what wasn't good about it could be solved by . . . well, for instance, writing an International Jogging Book.

Her thoughts turned now to the book idea, and her heart beat excitedly. She ambled slowly into the house. It was a small white clapboard house with green trim; it sat square on its lot and reminded all her friends of some house they had known in their youth, some southern summer cottage, some midwestern farmhouse or eastern beach house. This house of the Grays' was a fantasy junction of its own for bringing back some happy, yearning memory of one's youth.

A multiple-windowed porch ran along the front of the house, and one entered through glass French doors which were so unprowlerproof that Augusta not only did-n't lock them but usually left them open to the day. But this lowly location she lived in, this "undesirable neighborhood," did not attract thieves. It was the houses perched on mountain acreage or set in the canyons that consistently got robbed despite the protection of attack dogs, burglar alarms, direct wires to the police station, and electric fences the owners pretended were deer fences.

Curiously enough, the success of the robbers in Mill Valley allowed them to buy great quantities of hash and coke from the dealers, who flourished to such an extent that they became rich enough to buy Mill Valley houses in the desirable locations, where despite attack dogs, burglar alarms, etc., they soon got plundered them-selves.

Or so Augusta liked to think.

As she passed through the French doors she heard Val say, "Where's Mom?" and Lee answer, "Probably watch-ing the cherry tree," which made her smile, envisioning herself watching not the blossoms but the sturdy trunk.

The porch was alive with plants, and a new rug from the People's Republic of China released the fresh, subtle scent of straw into the green air that was tremulous with fronds. Another set of French doors opened onto a di-ning room which was presided over by a magnificent oil still life by Millicent Tomkins. Further along the porch, more French doors opened to the living room, furnished with only one L-shaped couch and a Parsons table set on a Berber rug. The rest of the room held books, piano, more plants, Nanao lithographs, and a Humble watercolor. The floors were golden oak.

At this point the house began to falter in its fantasticalness, as if the original builder had run out of money halfway; for as one got to the back of the building, there were only one and a half bedrooms, one bathroom, and an unmodernized kitchen. No matter. Beyond the backyard was a barnlike garage; in the first years in the house, while the girls gallantly camped out on the porch or crammed into the half-bedroom (really sort of a laundry room), Augusta and they sneaked behind Duke's back and built two big bedrooms in the garage—of which more later.

As Augusta washed the lettuce and spinach for the salad, she realized that despite the sublime moment beneath the cherry blossoms, she felt crabby.

"Will you chop the parsley for the sauce?" she asked Val.

"No, I don't want to."

"Then get out of the kitchen," Augusta snapped. "Get out of my way then."

She felt very irritable, and her ears were making funny crackling noises, and her heart hurt and her legs ached. She thought of the suicidal man whom jogging had transformed and wondered if the opposite might not happen with her, so that whereas previously she had moved serenely through life, with jogging, she would become bitchy and suicidal.

Now, with jogging, life will become hellish, she decided. Instead of going about waving and smiling at people, I will gesticulate wildly. I will be transformed from a happy housewife into the town scold.

Val returned to the kitchen and announced she'd cook the entire clam sauce if Augusta would chop the parsley.

"Deal," said Augusta, pleased.

Enter Duke.

A big hello for his three girls, a kiss for Augusta, and a hug for Lee, not Val.

It appeared he favored Lee over Val until the day he said sadly to Augusta, "Soon I won't be able to hug Lee anymore; she is getting to be such a big girl." Augusta was shocked to realize that some ancient puritan ethic was at work here which ruled that a father did not hug his daughter once she hit puberty, or the ogre Incest would raise its horrible head.

Bosoms or no, he did favor Lee. She *was* his favorite. They adored each other.

Duke's real name was Howard. He received his noble soubriquet at Princeton, quite a compliment for a poor boy on the GI bill, but he had about him an air of command, elegance, pure breeding, and confidence that comes of ancient lineage and inexhaustible funds—or in his case, from the fortuitous crossbreeding of Czech and Irish immigrants, youthful indifference to money, and the joy of university life after thirty degrees below in Korea.

A tall, well-built, blue-eyed man with luxuriant dark hair, at fifty, his face was baleful in repose but still raffish when he smiled. His business was in San Francisco. He called himself a fruit peddler, and Augusta could not rid herself of the picture of Duke selling apples out of a truck at some splendid scenic spot (such a nice picture, really), but in fact he was a fruit broker, in the very ticklish and exacting business of exporting fresh produce to the Orient. Now, in the spring, was a particularly harrowing time for him as he dispatched men to the valleys to try to ascertain which crops would be ready when, how bountiful they would be, and therefore how much they would cost and how many refrigerator cars he should line up on the freighters going west to the East.

Duke cracked a Coors and lay down on the couch with the evening paper. Presently Augusta joined him, perched on the back of the couch, and said, "Duke, I have a wonderful idea!"

"Just a minute."

She contained herself until he finished the article and looked up from his paper to say, "What's your idea?"

"Well," said Augusta, feeling a bit breathless with excitement, "it's an International Jogging Handbook, a guide to jogging areas in the capital cities of the world. You see . . ."

"It's been done."

Augusta looked at him, flabbergasted, the breathlessness knocked out of her, not because she believed for a minute that the book had been done, but because he would want to deflate her so mercilessly.

"Where have you seen a book of this nature?" she asked, her voice trembling although she was trying to be cool.

"I don't know. Somewhere. I've heard about it."

"You've heard it here, that's where. *That's* your somewhere. You've no doubt heard me muse about it. I am quite sure such a book does not now exist," she said stiffly.

"*Esquire* did an article on San Francisco, where to get a haircut, shoeshine, where to jog . . . "

"An article in *Esquire* on San Francisco is not a guide to jogging in international capitals."

"Okay, okay, never mind then. Suppose there isn't such a book; there's no market for one either."

"What do you mean? Everyone's crazy for jogging. There's all kinds of books on jogging, aerobics . . . "

"How many people are joggers who also travel around the world?"

"All the big-deal businessmen, that's who. And government people, diplomats! It would be a paperback book, you see"—Augusta's voice grew warm in spite of herself as she recaptured her enthusiasm—"and they could pick it up in airports or perhaps it could be distributed through corporations, consulates, the House of Representatives. Corporations are encouraging their employees to jog now, instead of drink."

"Augusta," Duke sighed with exasperation. "There just aren't that many international businessmen, and when you break it down to the number among them who jog . . . "

"Well, you see, I had also planned to make it a lively, readable book so that it would be a joy to read regardless. I suppose I could begin with a national jogging book, although that wouldn't be as much fun to research. I had thought we might go around the world together, you and I."

"Augusta!" Now his eyes were rolling about in his

head, suggesting the difficulty he was experiencing having to talk to a retarded person. "Augusta, I am a working man. I cannot leave my jog . . . my job for the amount of time it would take." He groaned and sputtered. "Do you have any idea how long it would take to research such a thing and how much money it would cost? Do you understand that I have to support this family?"

"Naturally I planned to get an advance on the book."

"No one is going to give you five cents for that idea." He rustled his paper to show how anxious he was to get back to it or, more likely, to get away from the conversation. "Not five cents!"

"Well, suppose they did. Would you come with me?"

"No."

"It would be such fun. You could stop smoking and run with me. It would be so good for your heart and blood pressure."

"My heart is fine. There's nothing wrong with my heart."

Almost nothing. He'd had a slight heart attack a year ago, but he refused to admit that it was one. He was the only person she knew who had not even *tried* to stop smoking. If someone tentatively suggested that he might well die a painful death from lung cancer, he said, "Yes, and I might get hit by a truck too." As for his ever-burgeoning belly, he patted it affectionately and said, "It's a sign of prosperity."

Now he was back with his paper, but he looked up to say, "Anyhow, I *hate* to run. I've always hated running, even when I was young." He said it with so much venom that it was as if she were asking him to go abroad with her to eat worms.

"If I do get the money, won't you please come?" she begged him. Actually, Augusta had a good idea of where she would get the money.

"No," he said.

Augusta went to plunge the spaghetti into boiling water. She was not daunted by this exchange with Duke. He'll want to come, she thought. It will be wonderful. It was as if she hadn't heard a word he said.

Instead of going for the spaghetti in the drawer, she went for the Scotch bottle in the cupboard.

"It happens every night," Val commented casually.

"What does?"

"Daddy comes home, you have a little talk with him, then you come to the kitchen and pour yourself a straight Scotch."

"It has nothing to do with your father. I love Scotch. Anyhow, it's not every night and it's only one. Why, this is my first drink this week." Augusta got out the ice.

"Today's Monday, Mom."

"So it is." Augusta stood looking woefully at the Scotch bottle.

"There is such a thing," said Val, "as a one-drink-a-night alcoholic."

"I suppose you saw a film on that at school too."

"No, I read about it."

"Humph." Augusta sadly put the bottle away. "Okay. Anyway, if I'm going to be a runner—and I am—I shouldn't drink whiskey. Water I guess, lots of water."

Val poured her a glass of water and handed it to her, smiling.

Augusta smiled back. "Maybe I'll give up talking to your father, too."

# 4

# . . . . . *Money*

AUGUSTA loved Duke. He was the only man she had
ever loved. If there were times when she contemplated
taking a lover just to see what it would be like with
another man, the times passed and she didn't, not find-
ing anyone to approach Duke in physical attractiveness,
charm, and intelligence. True, he was not as attractive
and charming as he had been ten years ago, but feelings
of love from the past can color the present.

She knew Duke was as faithful to her as she was to
him, that he was loyal, hardworking, a man of his word,

honest, a loving father; but she wished very much that they would do more things together, be more companionable. For years she had striven toward this end.

For instance, a few months ago she had signed them up for a weekly Badminton Night. Because he had been a champion player in high school, she believed that she had finally found a sport for them to share. But either he had to work each Badminton Night, or he was too tired. On Badminton Night of the fourth week, when he blithely said he wouldn't go, Augusta, shaken by a gust of sincere emotion, said tearfully, "All right, I give up. I have tried and tried to find something we can both enjoy doing together, but I see that you will never join me. All right then, Duke, you go your way and I'll go mine. I give up. This is the end. I'll *never* ask you to do something with me again. Never!"

Whereupon, instead of being struck with remorse, asking her forgiveness, and deciding to go to Badminton Night after all, he was overcome with boyish glee. He leapt in the air! He did a little dance! He grinned from ear to ear and said, "Hooray! I'm free! I'm free!"

So that Augusta, in despair, went further and said, "You can get a television set"—she had banned it from the house since Val was born—"and you can just watch television the rest of your life. Live vicariously. Become a vegetable."

More dancing and cheers. "Oh, boy, television. Val, Lee, we can get television at last! Whoopee!"

Worsted, Augusta went alone to Badminton Night. But she had to admire his spirit. If only she too could embrace the idea of freedom. But she didn't want freedom.

She wanted to have a wonderful marriage. Which is why she didn't give up as promised, and tried again with the jogging book idea.

And there was the time, not long ago at all, a matter of weeks, when Duke had been shouting at her for not cleaning the bathroom, for leaving a bottle of lotion on the sink, or a toothbrush, or possibly both. He shouted at her and swore irrationally, getting red-faced from his high blood pressure, saying, for instance, "This place is a shithouse!" and worse (she often thought there was no one more foulmouthed than a Princeton man), so that Augusta flared up.

"Very well, I'm sick of this treatment. I'm going to find another man. I'm going to find a man who will adore me, whose face will light up when he sees me, who will hug me and love me and not shout at me and expect me to be a cleaning woman, a servant, a char, and treat me like a dog. We will be equals, he and I, and life will be one grand sweet song!"

Val, who had been listening with interest to this exchange between her parents, said, "Dream on, Mom, dream on."

Augusta did dream on, but not of another man. She still dreamed of an ideal marriage with Duke. Hope was easily rekindled in her.

A few days after their disappointing discussion regarding the jogging idea, they had this conversation on the telephone.

"Oh, I feel so good, Duke. I've just been jogging at the track."

"You have? When did you start jogging?"

"Wednesday, when I got this idea for our book. I thought I'd better start preparing for it. Do you know I can go a mile in ten minutes? That's walking some of the time, of course. I can only run about half a mile nonstop."

"Now, you be careful, Augusta," he said with real concern. "I don't know if this is good for you. It isn't like you. You should stick to your tennis."

"But it's so hard to find someone to play with these days, and getting a free court is such a hassle. And this is so easy; it doesn't take any time at all—only half an hour out of your day, and that's not every day. How I wish you would join me in it. It's so good for you. I've been reading about aerobics today. Did you know that much of fatigue is simply caused by the body's not getting enough oxygen? Exercise makes you feel *less* tired, not more."

"Hummmmn," he said. Augusta thrilled to realize it was an interested hum, not a dubious one. On such crumbs did she feed her hopes: undubious hums.

"Are you coming home for supper? I've made minestrone."

"No, I have to work late, but I'll have a bowl when I get home. I love your soup."

"Good. I'll get up and join you. We'll have a midnight meal together. Meanwhile I'm going to bed with Anthony Trollope."

"That sounds pretty racy."

She laughed. "See you later, then. I love you."

"I love you, Augusta."

A marriage like any other, with ups and downs and sideways, based on a continuum of love.

But, as in all marriages, there's this sticky business of Money.

Augusta often thought that no one had ever done a proper study of the factors that form one's feelings towards money, and that they should have. What a moving force money is—much greater than the sexual urge, and look at all the books on sex! Money. Not a book on how to spend it, how to play the market, how to buy real estate, commodities, or options—no! A real analytical psychological probe of *feelings* about money was the book indicated.

Now, take Duke. When she accused him under her breath of being tighter than a cow's ass in the fly season, he retorted mildly, "Not so. I am a generous fellow. Generous, I might say, to a fault."

And he seemed to believe this.

Why, then, Augusta wondered, am I in debt?

Duke simply never had given Augusta (he allowanced her) enough money to live on. He paid the mortgage and his own daily expenses, and Augusta paid for everything else from her allowance: utilities, repairs, medical, dental, clothes, food, phone, etc., etc. And there had never, never been enough.

Over the years she had scraped and skimped and fiddled and owed and paid out token amounts to appease the merchants and gone through terrible, humiliating scenes in which she begged for more money from Duke and was accused in return of mishandling the finances. When she thrust her carefully kept accounts before his eyes so that it would become crystal clear to him that she was in a helpless situation, he disregarded her, wishing to remain in the monetary fantasy junction of his mind.

She did not know what he earned or if he saved or if in truth he *was* "generous to a fault" with his friends in the city, at business lunches and dinners, or in his travels to the Orient. His business life was separate; she had never seen his office.

She did allow herself one indulgence, which was buying art. However, she knew her stuff, had a good instinct for modern art, and therefore never paid much for it. Even when she lapsed from contemporary art and bought three original Hokusai woodcuts one year, they were good ones, and now there was a boom in Japanese prints. Duke knew that she spent little on it and it gave her great pleasure, but he always threw it up to her during their Money Scenes.

These painful scenes no longer occurred. Augusta had discovered that if you owned a house, you could borrow on it. So she did. Secretly.

# 5

## . . . . . *Ephraim at Home*

WITH so many millions, Evalyn Ruth had none of these problems. She enjoyed managing her money and encouraging the millions to pile up, exulted in spending it, remembered vividly what it was like to have none at all. She never wearied of her wealth, loved her residences, jewels, clothes, food, and drink. She always had a bottle of Mumms in the cooler within reach. She loved to entertain, to travel, to luxuriate.

But what about Ephraim and money? He suggested to Evalyn that he was independently wealthy, but we have *40. . .*

seen that Evalyn was having one of her intuitive bull's-eyes when she suggested that the research for his books supported him—if indeed he even wrote books. He did. And his protagonist was an assassin. His writing provided him, not with money, but with a psychologically unique sublimation of a sublimation.

He lived in an expensive, architecturally undistinguished apartment complex on Strawberry Point, which is on Richardson Bay between Mill Valley and the Tiburon Peninsula. He had a view of Mount Tamalpais in Mill Valley, of Sausalito, a seaside town between Mill Valley and San Francisco, and of San Francisco itself. Ephraim liked to see exactly where he was.

His apartment was monastic and scrupulously clean. Its walls were white, the rugs reaching to them burnt orange. On the rugs was a bare minimum of well-designed furniture.

A Goldberg Variation soared out from stereo speakers, but otherwise the only thing that reflected Ephraim's personal taste was Oceanic art. Hanging on the walls was an outstanding selection of masks garnered from his travels in Melanesia and Polynesia—the only area he had ever visited for pleasure. His work had taken him all over the rest of the world, but never there, because until Quilp no one ever needed someone murdered in the South Pacific.

Ephraim was an assassin of dazzling abilities. Although he had been trained by the US government, he now operated free-lance, working for private citizens as well as for foreign governments. He was the master of search and destroy, which entails having to find the victim first, generally with little or no information to go on. Ephraim liked nothing better than a job which required him to kill a certain man whose current alias, description, and location were totally unknown. Perhaps all Ephraim would have to go on would be a code name or the facts pertaining to a crime or plot his victim-to-be had perpetrated. For the Israelis he had searched out Nazis living incognito in South America. For the Americans he had accomplished the most bizarre and difficult of hits. In September, for instance, he had had to find a psychic who, according to the Defense Department, had such powerful psychokinetic abilities that he could blow out the ARPA computer network—and had.

Over the years, Ephraim had hit for the Mafia, governments, and heads of corporations. He had never failed, and his pride on this front was enormous. He was a perfectionist, a loner—a lone perfectionist. Although a marksman and a karate expert, he was always interested in learning new ways to kill. And lately he had found himself drifting to the *aikido dojo* in the city, intrigued by the subtlety of the art.

He was thinking about this one morning shortly after his return from Fiji as he lay in a yellow velour robe, listening to Bach, slightly disturbed to find himself attracted to *aikido*, which is not the art of killing, or even defending, but of blending.

*Ai* meant harmony. Worse, it meant love.

With a languid gesture, Ephraim picked up the little booklet containing the words of the founder of *aikido*, Morihei Uyeshiba.

"*Aki*," he read, "is not a technique to fight with or defeat the enemy, it is the way *(budo)* to reconcile the world and make human beings one family."

This *budo* would put me out of a job, thought Ephraim.

O Sensei (the great master) went on to say, "The secret of *aikido* is to harmonize ourselves with the movement of the universe and bring ourselves into accord with the universe itself. He who has gained the secret of *aikido* has the universe in himself and can say 'I am the universe.' "

I like that. I would be glad to say "I am the universe." That is an attractive notion.

But was it attractive enough for him to allow himself into the discipline? Because if there was some inner flaw drawing him to *aikido*, he must search it out and destroy it. *Aikido* must make him stronger, not weaker.

He knew it was good for his body; the rolls and falls demanded a suppleness that karate didn't. As well, there was some magic involved.

He had seen a film of O Sensei, at eighty, taking on attackers—a frail old man handling a multiple assault from judo black belts. Ephraim had studied the pictures frame by frame, and there were seconds in which the master appeared to vanish entirely. In one frame he was on this spot. How, then, in the very next frame, could the old man be standing way over there while all his attackers had only moved infinitesimally?

The ability to vanish, Ephraim thought, would be extremely useful.

Not because he was so noticeable. He liked that about himself and believed that his very flamboyance created a shield of protection around him. This man could not be a killer, one would think, because he is too unusual-looking; he draws all eyes.

So does a magician, of course. He draws all eyes to himself to divert the audience from seeing what his hands are doing.

Ephraim got up and went to the window. A drought was scourging Marin County. The rainy season had passed the county by, and as a result, the hills looked particularly dead and colorless, especially after the luxuriance of Fiji's greenery and flowers.

He sat down and returned to the memoir of the master. Uyeshiba urged him not to think in terms of enemies, as this created a mind of discord which would defeat him from the first.

Done. He never thought in terms of enemies. He was not fighting a war, he was doing a job. However, if Uyeshiba wanted him to love, he must draw the line, even if it meant forfeiting the ability to be the universe.

"Do not look at the opponent's eyes or your mind will be drawn into his eyes. Don't look at his sword or you will be slain with his sword. Don't look at him or your spirit will be distracted. True *budo* is the cultivation of attraction with which to draw the whole opponent to you. All I have to do is to keep standing this way. Even standing with my back toward the opponent is enough. When he attacks, hitting, he will injure himself with his own intention to hit. I am one with the universe and I am nothing else. When I stand, he will be drawn to me. There is no time and space before Uyeshiba of *Aikido* . . . only the universe as it is."

That is how he is able to vanish—by eliminating time and space, by slipping away into the universe for the nonce, into a quark, perhaps.

"I am calm. I have no attachment to life or death."

I can say that of myself. I'm with you there. But you are calm because you have God and are one with the universe. I am calm because I feel I am perfect.

"Love is the guardian deity of everything. Nothing can exist without it. *Aikido* is the realization of love."

I don't know what you mean by love, Ephraim thought irritably.

"I don't know" was an expression that Ephraim never used, because it could be a cry of anguish, of helplessness, and he was never helpless or anguished. So, when he heard himself think "I don't know," he suspected that this *aikido*, this way, was not good for him.

But *nobody* knows what love is, he placated himself. He returned to the memoir, fascinated, drawn in.

What does he *think* he means by love? It's a word, just a word. Why does it have such power?

"I do not make a companion of men," said Uyeshiba.

Nor do I, old man. In many ways we understand each other.

"Who then do I make a companion of ? God."

Ah, there again we must have a parting of the *budo*.

"This world is not going well because people make companions of each other, saying and doing foolish things."

Right.

"*Aikido* leaves out any attachment."

Terrific.

Then there was more about love and God, so that Ephraim was constrained to lay down the book thinking, There must be a way to learn to vanish that precludes the realization of love or the companionship of God. I will go to the *dojo* for the practice without committing myself to the way. There are ten thousand different variations of throws. Why not learn them all? In the end all benefits come from mastery. Not God, no love. And talent, too, of course. Mastery and talent. Listen to old Bach.

Ephraim got dressed and put three satisfying hours in on his incredibly complex new novel.

After a light lunch he went down to swim in the pool. Two young girls watched him with slack-jawed admiration, but they made no move to attract him. They seemed to sense that he was not a "companion of men" or of women, that he was a totally inaccessible person.

# 6

# . . . . . *Augusta Gray, Heiress*

IF DUKE had ever allowed himself to entertain the notion that Augusta had a lover, or lovers, it would have been about a year ago when, as they walked together through the town, strange young men greeted her and she blushed, looked embarrassed, seemed guilty.

She *was* guilty. The young men were nonunion electricians and carpenters who had come to estimate the work that needed to be done on the garage—and that Augusta had secretly commenced.

Duke bought their house not because he liked it, as

Augusta did, but because it was cheap, and in his business he did not need to put up a front by having a fancy house or car to impress clients. His clients were across the seas. Nor did he care about his social "image." The Grays only entertained friends of whom they were fond.

But it was small, smaller than the apartment they had occupied in San Francisco. Even Duke saw this and said that it was small. However, the smallness of the house was redeemed by the largeness of the garage—almost a barn—and it was agreed that Duke would build two bedrooms there for the girls.

Augusta knew that Duke could build bedrooms. There was nothing Duke could not do—a man of many talents.

But would he?

She thought not. He was not a man who was happiest at his workbench. His mind took a more scholarly turn, and his body a more recumbent angle. He was disposed to ruminate in bed of a weekend with books, maps, and cigarettes. This was his paradise.

Toward the end of the first year in their new home, when Duke still hadn't gotten around to doing the work on the garage, Augusta began talking gently about hiring someone to do it. But Duke grew angry and forbade her. "You are on no account to hire anyone for anything. I'll do it. I have said that I'll do it, and I will."

But when?

Meanwhile, the girls found their living conditions intolerable. Their four years' difference in age was not conducive at this time to the growth of real intimacy. They and Augusta began to conspire. Perhaps they could build the bedrooms themselves?

No. They hadn't the knowledge or the training. But they could scout around and find some old doors and windows in the style of the house, and get Duke's project under way.

They drove far afield, to Cleveland Wrecking in a distant corner of San Francisco and to Sunrise Salvage in Berkeley. They found charming many-paned windows of wood, and from a friend they bought a fine sturdy door for a dollar. Did this inspire Duke to get going?

No.

Then Augusta learned about home improvement loans and quietly got one for five thousand dollars—a fifteen-year loan at eleven percent interest with a monthly payment of fifty-six dollars and eighty-three cents.

This sum, which she stashed in a separate checking account, allowed her not only to hire handymen, but to pay off all her outstanding bills and (this was the clever part) have money to spare for the loan payments as well as for her regular monthly bills.

It's hard to believe that two bedrooms were built in the garage behind Duke's back, but this is true. Major construction took place twenty feet away from his bedroom. He never went out to the garage, and the workers came by day when he was gone. The lumber and sheetrock were kept in the undisturbed part of the garage.

First an electrician came and rewired the joint. Then a carpenter put in the sturdy door and charming windows. Another carpenter raised two skeletons of walls so that each room would have the customary four.

Augusta, armed with a staple gun and suited up like a wasp exterminator (flesh covered, hands gloved, panes over her eyes—all against the ferocity of fiberglass) shot insulation into the spaces between the studs. She felt like a heroic figure. What a woman! There was nothing she could not do!

Except sheetrock. Oh, the heaviness of sheetrock! The endless pulling out of bent nails, the hammering in of straight ones and of thumbs. The unaccustomed muscle use: the right hand going into clawlike spasms from all the hammering. She did a terrible job. But the paint will cover it, she thought. At least there are walls now where previously there was air.

Slowly, slowly, the garage became a habitable place. After the sheetrocking, the girls spackled and sanded and painted. A final carpenter came and laid a floor over the cement and put a sliding door between the rooms. Val's yellow room got a gold rug, and Lee's bright blue room a green one. Wow! What colors. What rooms! A Room of One's Own, Virginia. And Augusta could now have the little half-room as a study—a half-room of one's own!

The work took five months. She was in constant fear of discovery—of Duke's fury. But somehow she trusted that if he didn't find out until it was all done, he could not be angry. Everyone loves a *fait accompli*.

But all of this took so much craft and wile, so much lying and sneaking, that it was a great strain on Augusta. She became a practiced deceiver, a crackerjack deceiver, but she wasn't happy about it. She hated it, was beseiged nightly by bad dreams because of it, and by day she had a hunted, skulking look. It was during this time that her agoraphobia began; so, although the girls got their bedrooms, Augusta lost her mind.

Needing a quote to guide her through this troubled time and having none in her store, Augusta went hopefully to her *Oxford Dictionary of Quotations.* She knew that the really guiding quotes were never found in books like these, interesting though they were. The guiding ones leapt out from some unexpected source and hit her right between the eyes, or some person like Count Dracula said them just when she was hardly attending.

There were twenty-two entries under *deceit* and *deceiving*, and after collating them, she obediently looked them up.

Isaiah, his words flying like thunderous cannonballs over her head, declared, "The heart is deceitful above all things, and desperately wicked!"

"If we say that we have no sin, we deceive ourselves and the truth is not in us," said the First Epistle General of Peter.

No, thought August, I'm not deceiving myself. I'm perfectly clear about myself.

(The truth was no longer in Augusta.)

She read what Bishop Joseph Butler was resigned to feel. "Things and actions are what they are, and the consequences of them will be what they will be; why then," he asked, "should we desire to be deceived?"

Could Duke possibly *desire* to be deceived? Augusta paused and pondered this stunning notion, which seemed attractive at first and then quite horrible. No, she thought, I would not like to think I was going through all this wretchedness only to follow some unconscious program he had laid out, some yearning for deceit from me. No, unthinkable! Never. Not Duke. And yet . . . ?

The other quotes were a lot of mush about deceitful lovers. Apparently none of the great thinkers had ever put the spotlight of their brains on the kind of deceiving woman who builds bedrooms behind her husband's back.

When the bedrooms were done and proudly displayed, was Duke mad? No. Was he, could he have been, pleased?

You bet. He had got two bedrooms for fifteen hundred dollars—raising the value of their property by ten big ones, at least—without, so to speak, leaving his bed. The man was a genius.

By way of pecuniary explanation, Augusta said she had borrowed fifteen hundred from Fidelity Savings and Loan which she would pay back when she got her inheritance.

For Augusta was an heiress. No thanks to her parents.

Her parents were dead, and her brother, Dana, was a rich man. After the death of her father, Augusta had been "cut off without a penny" by her mother. Her mother had forthrightly explained to Augusta that she was leaving the entire estate to her brother because, "I believe in primogeniture."

Maybe she did believe in primogeniture; this could have been true. It was certainly true that she didn't believe in Augusta, never had. They hadn't got along since the breast she decided not to suckle Augusta at after all. She didn't wean her, just took it away—wrenched it away. "It's not that I'm worried about the shape," she told her husband, Augusta's father. "It's just that this baby seems to like it too much; so greedy, she positively guzzles." For days—weeks!—Augusta howled with grief and desolation, which intensified her mother's dislike for her and set it for life.

(Augusta *was* a greedy baby, her mother *was* worried about her breast shape, *and* her mother was crazy.)

However, there was a recently expired aunt who had liked Augusta extremely well and who had kindly bequeathed fifty thousand dollars to her, not a vast sum— one couldn't live on the income from it, three thousand—but an awfully nice amount of money for a woman getting on to middle age who'd never had any money of her own and had all these money problems with her husband.

Now, in March, the will of her beloved aunt was *ostensibly* in the process of being probated, so that Augusta, to all outward appearances, did not yet have the money in hand.

When she was first informed of this remembrance she had been touched and pleased. What a windfall! What fun they would have with this money!

But Duke had already decreed that the money should be set aside for the girls' education (fortuitously Princeton had gone coed). Education of the Ivied kind now cost twenty-five thousand per child!

No good Augusta telling Duke that the Cal system provided as excellent an education as Princeton for a tenth of the cost. He knew that.

Very well, at least they could enjoy the yearly income from the money, couldn't they?

No. She must reinvest the dividends so the money could "build."

The money was in securities, and they had already

been apprised of which stocks they held. The aunt had died when the market was low, and now, the market was booming, had passed the thousand mark, and Augusta's portfolio read like the Dow-Jones average. Imagine Duke's joy! They had made five thousand dollars in the last few months alone! (On paper, that is.)

Now, in bed of a weekend, he was no longer deep into history books and atlases, swathed in a cumulus of smoke. No, now there was the phut-phut-phut of the calculator, the rustle-rustle-rustle of the *Wall Street Journal,* the swish-swish-swish of hands rubbing together, vocal expulsions of glee.

"Union Carbide up two points since Thursday," he called to Augusta in the kitchen. "Do you know that St. Regis has doubled since your aunt died? It's incredible. The wildest speculation couldn't hope for such a gain. And now Exxon and Standard Oil Indiana are really taking off. We haven't got one stock that has gone down. As for General Motors . . . "

Augusta could not share his excitement, even felt distaste. She had a deep distrust of the stock market that perhaps only an art lover can have. Augusta loved Duke, her children, and Art. She didn't love money; she only needed a little more of it. She didn't love the stock market, didn't understand it at all, only knew that it had done incalculable harm to people whose fortunes, big and small, had been eroded by it. She was the sort of woman who would keep her money, if she had any, under the mattress. She did not trust banks either, and she believed that most bankers were crooks. Her worst spells of agoraphobia occurred in banks, and she thought this could well be because of the bad vibes or emanations of evil that inundated her senses in banks.

No, she could not share Duke's joy. Too bad. This was something they could "share," could "do" together, but to Augusta, watching the paper make them money "on paper" was neither companionable nor exhilarating. Where was the satisfaction? Where was the sweat?

Running! thought Augusta in March, hot in pursuit of her jogging book idea. Running is where the sweat is.

# 7

## . . . . . *Aikido of Tamalpais*

RUNNING, thought Ephraim, is so boring.

Nevertheless, he ran three to six miles a day, since he knew it could do for his heart and lungs what his martial art could not. As with a dancer or an athlete, the well-being of his body determined the duration of his career —and he was as disciplined as the best of them. Like Nureyev, Shorter, Ali, he too, in his work, was world class.

It was boring, but he liked it because he liked anything that made him better, that honed him. He liked it because it was part of his overall discipline for himself, his way.

He ran a route he had mapped out around the marshes of Richardson Bay. The air was good, and no one else seemed to come there. Sometimes a great blue heron or a snowy egret rose up out of the marsh on wondrous wings, but Ephraim took no special notice.

(Augusta, running sometimes on the marsh with Lee, seeing such a bird, would stop immediately and stand transfixed, dazzled, her hand pressed to her heart, which her heightened sense of wonder and beauty caused rapidly to thump. She was beginning to distinguish her three different rapid-heart-thumps: anaerobic, agoraphobic, ecstatic.)

But Ephraim took no special notice unless it was to classify (heron, egret, etc.) just as he might do for the growth (blackberry, lupin, manzanita, skunk cabbage) or the clouds (cirrus today with a slight building up of cumulus).

Another reason for running was to keep in touch with weather and weather conditions—keep a sensitivity to them, keep alive the primitive response to the rhythms of nature. The ability to guess the day's weather could make all the difference to a satisfactory hit arrangement. He had nothing but contempt for the weathermen, convinced that they never went outside except to cover the space from car to darkroom to look at their satellite picture of the latest storm building up over the Pacific that would dissipate as soon as they reported it.

In addition, moving his own body through the spacetime continuum kept his sense of distance, or range, in tune.

Ephraim brought the same intelligence and dimensionality to stillness that he brought to running. For an hour each day he practiced hatha-yoga. He practiced every possible physical position and learned to hold it until the muscles screamed for release. This stretched his muscles and kept them limber, but essentially it taught him to be still, as still as an animal, to have as much control of the autonomic nervous system as of the voluntary.

The rapidly running forward, the holding still, the whirling leaps and falls of *aikido*—these three disciplines made his body the perfect instrument. There was nothing it could not do.

Except one thing: hold another human body to his own, enter that body, let his pelvis express its own amazing rhythmic possibilities of speed and motion through the continuum, and of endurance, power, fine sensing, and tuning. To let the sweat stream forth from every pore with the fiery flush and flash of release followed by a kind of stillness he had never known, a kind of heavenly immobility no yogi could ever show him, a letting go, a letting go . . .

Ephraim could not do that. No.

He was twenty-seven years old and a virgin.

Later in the day, after his run, his yoga, and his writing, he set out for the city for a couple of hours at the *dojo*. He got into his car, a dark green E type, and paused before igniting the engine.

He had heard of a new *dojo* that had opened right in downtown Mill Valley. Why not check it out? Apparently

three black belts, two men and a woman, had pooled
their resources and opened a school in the top floor of
the building where the town newspaper went to press.
He rarely went into Mill Valley proper, preferring to
keep a low profile in his own town, but he could park his
car some blocks away, wear his *gi*, and be just another
student wandering in from the street.

He did just that. A sign on the door of Aikido of
Tamalpais said to go around to the rear, and here he
went up a long flight of iron steps on the outside of the
building to an open door from which issued the familiar
thumping sounds of mat falls.

Ephraim stood at the door feeling well pleased. The
room was large, high-ceilinged, well lit, with a blue mat
and rough wooden walls painted white. There was a long
mirror at the far wall. Two sides were all windows, and
on the other wall, displayed with perfect simplicity, was
a framed black-and-white photograph of O Sensei. Near
the entrance was a small, open office space for the school
business, on the counter of which was a vase of deep
purple iris.

Ephraim stepped into the *dojo*.

He would remember taking that step. Later, looking
back, Ephraim would see that this was where it all began
for him. But even at the time he had an uneasy sense of
its importance—an intimation of karma—so that he
paused at the threshold. He paused and would have
turned and departed except that he realized that the very
act of pausing, framed in the doorway, a startling appearance, made him memorable. He would be engraved on

the memories of those within if he appeared only to disappear. Who was that? they would wonder. Did you see him? An apparition! Red-haired and about eight feet tall.

So he stepped in.

# 8

## .....*Evalyn at Home,*
### *or*
## *What Money Can't Buy*

EVALYN returned from New Zealand to her mansion in Sacramento in high spirits. She was cheerfully greeted by her cook, chauffeur, maid, housekeeper, personal secretary, and attack dog—five females and one bitch—cheerfully because they were paid to be cheerful as well as efficient, and even the attack dog, a Doberman, seemed to understand this. But they were actually all quite sad, because it had been such a heavenly time for them while Evalyn was away, especially for Nancy O'Hara, Evalyn's secretary and most intimate friend, the one who most consistently had to endure personal contact with Evalyn.

We have seen Evalyn in Fiji at her most attractive and charming, but we haven't had to live with her. She was charming, but she was also tempermental, paranoid, and cruel. It was not for nothing that Nancy, a slim, delightful, witty Irish girl when she came to Evalyn ten years ago, now weighed three hundred pounds.

Why did she stay with Evalyn, then? Why? Why was Augusta still with Duke? Nancy at least got paid. And lived in luxury.

The chauffeurs took the ten matched pieces of Louis Vuitton to her bedroom, where the maid unpacked. The cook set out the Mumms and a selection of hors d'oeuvres on the coffee table in the living room, where the housekeeper had built a fine fire—which Evalyn demanded every evening despite the warmth of Sacramento. She liked looking at it. She had promised herself at twenty that she would never be cold again, and she hadn't been; she always held her champagne glass by the stem, so that even her fingers, since twenty, had not been cold.

The large, high-ceilinged living room was carpeted in a thick chocolate-brown. The few pieces of furniture were white, beige, and comfortable. There was one benjamina tree, one pretty good Picasso oil painting, and one very beautiful gold-framed mirror. Her decor, like her clothes, was tasteful and unexceptional.

"Well, Nancy." She smiled, raising her glass.

"Welcome home," said Nancy in her mellifluous voice, holding some liver pâté on a cracker poised before her

mouth. "You look marvelous, Evalyn." She placed the
tidbit in her mouth and chewed slowly and pleasurably.
"We missed you very much," she lied effortlessly. Nancy's countenance was almost always inscrutably agree-
able, and when she smiled it was enchanting.

"Do I look different to you, Nancy?"

"Different? Well, you are beautifully tanned, but you
are always tanned. You seem relaxed." This, too, was a
lie; Evalyn was never relaxed, but she very much liked
to be told that she looked it. "You have something of the
appearance of . . . "

"Yes?"

"The cat that swallowed the canary, as if you had put
through some canny business deal."

"But that would not be different," Evalyn pouted.
"This is *different*, Nancy. What is the only thing I don't
have in life? The only thing money cannot buy? Think!"

So many things came to Nancy's mind that she was astonished. However, she didn't dare say any of them.

"You are afraid to say, am I right? But I like my little
guessing game. Come on, play."

"Well . . . " Nancy helped herself to some caviar.
"Children?" she suggested.

"Phooey. Money can buy children, and you know I
don't like them. No, a child is something I do not desire.
This is something infinitely desirable and something I
had thought to be . . . do I dare to say . . . beyond my
powers?"

Nancy smiled. "It would be out of character to say
that, certainly."

"That is very funny, Nancy," Evalyn said dryly.

Nancy sometimes allowed herself a joke at Evalyn's expense, but one of the things money couldn't buy Evalyn was a sense of humor.

"Play," said Evalyn.

"Well, it couldn't be a husband. You have always had more suitors than you could handle, and you've turned them all down."

"No, it is not a husband. God knows, money can buy husbands. Rest assured there would be a miraculous disappearing act of suitors if I suddenly became poverty-stricken."

"I give up. I just can't imagine anything that is beyond your powers, Evalyn," said Nancy with her seeming guilelessness.

"Then I will tell you," said Evalyn decisively. She knocked back her glass of champagne and poured another. For just a split second, Nancy saw the face of a vulnerable, half-starved little German girl, and was moved by it.

But it was the mature Evalyn who looked directly at Nancy and said, "Orgasm."

Nancy didn't know if she was surprised or not. She had not put it on her secret list of things money couldn't buy for Evalyn. She guessed she had always thought orgasm was a given. It had been given to her, at any rate, in the days when men were more important than food, or as important. But if it wasn't a given, how did you get it? Not with money, it seemed, or Evalyn would have a stockpile of it. No, money could not buy orgasms.

Evalyn was looking keenly at Nancy. "Laugh and I will kill you." She lit a cigarette and stuck it in her holder. "I am telling you what I have not told any living person. I have never had an orgasm in my life until this month. I am forty-six years old. I had convinced myself that this was not important, that perhaps it was not even desirable, for wouldn't orgasm make me vulnerable, place me in someone's power? Yes, I was right. This is true. I am vulnerable now, and I am in the power of this man, for he is the only man who can make me happy. Luckily he is a nice man. Incredibly, of all the men, he is the only one who appears totally uninterested in my wealth. Like me, he is a confirmed bachelor. But imagine, Nancy, forty-six years old and this was the first time! When I was forty and began to feel life slipping by and began to be aware that there was more and more talk about this mystery, more and more writing about it, it occurred to me I could be helped, perhaps with psychotherapy. But I have never been able to ask for help, even if I am paying for it. And what a can of worms analysis would open in me!

"I have heard of women's groups—there is one in Berkeley. Women who suffer from this . . . this deformity! . . . meet together and help each other out. Can you imagine *me* joining such a group?

"Again I convinced myself it didn't matter. I was too old anyhow, and every other pleasure was available to me. But of course it became the only thing that I desired.

"Now, by the grace of God—and I think I can mention Him in this connection—I have found this happiness through this man who is so talented in . . . tenderness."

"I'm glad for you, Evalyn. I look forward to meeting him."

"You will meet him soon. I have invited him to

Acapulco the middle of April. Sacramento is too dull to have him here. I leave it to you to correspond with the Mexicans in your excellent Spanish so that the villa can be put in readiness. Say we are arriving the first of April so that it will be ready for sure by the tenth."

"Very well," Nancy sighed. She disliked Acapulco, where because of the language difficulty, she must attend Evalyn constantly. Here in Sacto she could sometimes get away—as long as she left a number where she could be reached.

Still, the orgasmic Evalyn might be a wonderful change for the better, a transformation! As long as the man was going to be available, that is. What if she became hopelessly centered on this man, dependent on him, and he chose not to answer her beck and call like the rest of them—answer cheerfully, too—what then?

But Evalyn would be her most charming with him, and he would grow attached to her and to her great wealth. And she was clever; she had her ways to cleave people to her. She had her immutable ways, some of which didn't bear thinking about too deeply.

"I wuv him. Me wuvs 'im." Evalyn sometimes unaccountably lapsed into baby talk, often just before saying something particularly vicious. "Evalyn vewee happy, Nancy."

"That's great, Evalyn."

There was a silence between them. Evalyn sighed and lay back against the couch cushions. Nancy masticated caviar, onion, and egg, and wondered if Evalyn said *wuv* because she was embarrassed to say the word *love*. I'd be more embarassed to say wuv, Nancy decided. Vewee embarassed.

"Call Jane," Evalyn said. "Have her clear away in here, and we'll have supper by the fire. Afterwards we'll go over any important business that's transpired in my absence." She looked at Nancy distastefully. "On second thought, have cook bring my supper to the study. There are times when I just can't bear watching you eat yourself to death, and I think tonight is one of them. Have you thought any more about that stomach removal operation?"

"No, I haven't."

"Well, do."

Nancy sighed. She guessed the orgasmic Evalyn wasn't going to be a transformation after all.

# 9

## . . . . . *The First International Jogging Route*

ON APRIL Fools' Day evening, Duke said, "As an alternative to going around the world together, would you like to come with me to Carson City for the weekend? We can see the Sierras while there's still snow on them, do a little gambling, and have a brief change."

"Sounds great. I'd love to. But the Mercedes would never make it over the mountains."

Duke frowned as he always did when his car's performance was impugned. "I put two new front tires on it. The shimmy's gone now, and it's a delight to drive. It's a champion!"

68. . .

"I wonder why you couldn't have done that months ago so that I could have delighted in driving it, instead of feeling I was subjecting the girls and myself to mortal danger every time I got in it. It really wounds me that you would fix the car for this trip but not for me."

"Augusta, you know that you never drive anywhere except the two miles to town at twenty-five miles an hour."

"Maybe I would go farther afield if I felt safe doing so."

"I doubt it very much. You are a stay-at-home by nature."

Yes, she thought sadly to herself, because I am so afraid of open spaces.

That very day she had made a valiant attempt to go to town alone, setting off as soon as she had done her morning chores. The driving there alone wasn't too bad. Even a hated car creates a comforting cave, or carapace, to feel safe in. She thought that the best chance for a successful trial run as a solitary would be to go to the library, where, surrounded by the benignity of books, she would not feel alone and unprotected.

Before getting out of the car, she relaxed her body and mind. When she stepped out, she breathed deeply, reminding herself that the library was her home away from home, an enchanted, kindly place.

She entered through the glass doors and browsed calmly among the stacks, every so often tucking a book in the crook of her arm. Calmly, calmly she browsed, but a tinkling in her brain was beginning. Wires were being pulled, broken, exposed. The tinkle was becoming a jangle. The unease was invading her, slowly building to a panic. Fear flashed through her. Her stomach began to heave with nausea, her jangling head began to whirl.

I have only to put my head down, she thought. That sound of cowbells is only the noise of blood leaving my brain—purely a clinical sound. I have only to put my head between my knees to get that blood going back where it belongs. Or better, I've only to lay my whole body down and I'll be fine. It is impossible to faint lying down; I have it on a doctor's authority.

But the idea of lying down on the library floor— astonishing the gathered citizenry—filled her with a larger panic. When one panics, there is a natural inclination to flee, to run like hell from what scares you, not to lie down in the midst of it. Augusta moved rapidly to the door. She dropped the books on a table and ran out of the library.

If only I can get to the car. If only I don't faint before I get to the car.

She opened the car door and threw herself over the front seats with her head hanging to the floor. She did not lose consciousness. Far from deserting her, her senses were stupefyingly heightened. Her ears roared like volcanic eruptions, a kaleidoscope of dazzling colors whirled around her. She lost all strength, all sense of time and place, but was overwhelmed by sight and sound and a scent as sharp and metallic as a Toledo blade— which must have been the scent of fear.

Augusta came to herself covered with sweat, enfeebled in body, but strangely—and this was always true—serene in her mind. She was always left with a lovely, light serenity, as if her mind and body had undergone a gigantic spring cleaning; or as if God, that great pugilist in the sky, had used her for a punching bag to train for a big match and then, as recompense, given her a state of grace to carry on with.

God loves me. There is a reason for all this. It is worth the fainting to have this exalted after-feeling.

In this way she glamorized and made tolerable this horror in her life.

"You're right," Augusta said now to Duke this April Fools' Day night. "I am a stay-at-home. Or I was. I'm changing. Presently I'm going around the world, and you are still cordially invited."

"Meanwhile, how about Carson City?"

"Great," she smiled. "I'd love to go with you."

In Carson City, Nevada, Augusta wrote out her first jogging route. Granted, Carson City wasn't one of the great international capitals of the world, but it *was* the capital of Nevada (population thirty thousand including county) and would do for a practice run toward bigger and better capitals.

She went out for a run on Sunday while Duke, who had been gambling until six in the morning, was still asleep—he virtually had just gone to sleep. When she returned to their room, this is what she wrote from her notes:

CARSON CITY, NEVADA, USA, JOGGING ROUTE

If you can find your way through the lobby of the Ormsby House—for it is not a lobby at all as you know it, but a casino nightclub and slot-machine palace with a small reception desk in a far, dark corner looking like an old tintype of a reception desk pasted onto the screen of a bad technicolor movie—then get out, if you can, through the side entrance and commence your run thus: Turn left on West Sixth towards the vista of snow-covered mountains, then turn right onto South Nevada. Here and for most of the rest of the run you will be on grass and dirt, which are preferable to gravel, macadam, asphalt, terrazzo, brick, and reinforced concrete. But watch out for the low-growing branches of the catalpa (or possibly linden).

Turn left toward the mountains again on West Fifth, right on South Division, where the trees are poplars for sure, with branches so vertical you can relax and run upright past charming little houses for three blocks. Left on West Second to check out a church, then, realizing it looks better at a distance, veer off, turning right on South Minnesota. Right on King Street presents a view of the silver cupola of the handsome state capital building. Left on Division towards three more churches, fetching up at the tiny, elegant, slender-spired white Episcopal Church, worth the whole run. Right on Robinson takes you to Carson, the main drag of the town, bordered by a blend of architectural monstrosities new and old.

If you expect to feel embarrassed jogging down the main street of a capital, you won't in Carson City, where no one is abroad at any hour. No one ever walks, let alone runs, in Nevada. If they do get out of their cars, it is only to step directly inside a casino—so you will be the only one on the sidewalk, I assure you.

On the corner of Robinson is the Nevada State Museum. Jog right on Carson, past the State Library and County Courthouse. At Proctor, cross Carson and go a block on to Plaza so as to run by the nice stone ruin and awful wedding chapel—"Weddings 24 Hours a Day!" Now run onto the grounds of the state capital building. Here you will be in no doubt as to the names of the branches you are ducking, as the trees are thoughtfully labeled. The Ormsby House is in view now, so slow down to walk off your run. Amble by the new, outstandingly ugly Nevada State Senate and Assembly, cross the street to the hotel, go in and try to find the elevators—which are more dimly recessed than the reception desk, as the management has a horror of any of the clientele ever leaving the tables and going to bed.

Augusta read over her first jogging route and felt discouraged. What a totally asinine jogging route!

For one thing, she had named (she counted) twelve different streets. Twelve! Who is going to remember them all? The jogger isn't going to want to commit all these names to memory before his run, nor does he want to carry the route to read as he's running.

And all those turns! There were (she counted) six right turns, four left turns, and one veer. This was absurd. Why not toss the jogger in a labyrinth and be done with it?

And why worry the runner with all the branches? Are the names of trees important (or even interesting) to the runner? Is this a jog or nature walk? Is he, like you, going to be a church fancier who runs towards any spire or steeple pricking erotically through the treetops? He will do his sight-seeing another time, thank you. Right now he is only wanting to have his daily run.

Why not say something about the wonderful air? Probably your joggers will never again run in a city with such fabulous, crystalline, breathable air. Every other capital is going to be so smoggy that you are probably doing people an injury to encourage them to run there.

This made Augusta feel more discouraged. A report had just come out saying that cancer was caused not by viruses but by our very own man-made environment—something Percival Pott could have told them in 1775 in his report on scrotum cancer among chimney sweeps, thought Augusta. Something pretty environmental to be deduced from that, what?

So Augusta felt discouraged about the environment, her jogging book, and her marriage. She had a moment of clarity, of truth being in her, as she often seemed to after running, and she thought to herself: Face it. Duke is never going to come with me around the world to write this book. Even if he did, he would sleep all day as he is doing now (she glanced bitterly at his recumbent form) and be out all night without me at the gaming tables being "generous to a fault."

Probably he is quite right that no one needs this book, but . . . *I* need it.

Suddenly she was struck by a wonderful, depression-dispelling thought. She had gone all over Carson City alone.

Alone!

She stood up and held the thought carefully, like something so fragile it would smash if she exulted too soon, so delicate it might dissolve if she looked at it too closely, might prove to be an illusion, a delusion. But she could not contain herself. Her spirit exploded with joy. ALONE! Alone, alone, I've ventured abroad alone! she sang to herself. I did it! I can do it!

This is incredible, she thought, truly overwhelmed. I'm well. I'm a well person. I am normal. I can cope. I will never have to be certified and committed—a fear which I never dared to express even to myself, but which encouraged me to keep my disease such a dark secret from everyone (Duke) so that I might remain free. Especially since Duke wouldn't want to spend the money on a nice nursing home and would put me in the state asylum. Not really. Just joking. Ha-ha.

But it is true, she thought, that I was secretly afraid. There is insanity in my family, a rampant strain of it. They say it can't be inherited. Hogwash. It's congenital as hell, insanity—a DNA special, second only to hemophilia and tightwaddery (but not scrotum cancer), and for sure I inherited my lunacy from Mother, who never bothered to hide it in the least but capitalized on it so that she never had to lift a hand to do anything in her life except to go frivolously about to all the lovely watering spots of the world. If you're rich, it's fun to be insane. Your madness gives you that much more power over people—no one can say you nay. Although the occasional series of electric shock treatments couldn't have been any fun, poor woman. Anyhow, I somehow believed this agoraphobia jag would leave me mysteriously. It did descend upon me one day without notice and, like the man who came to dinner, broke its leg and stayed, lingering on and on in my brain or spine ganglia or amorphous area of soul—wherever it is that madness lodges. Maybe I jogged it free of me. Maybe it couldn't stand the running; that's the only thing I've done different. That, and I've become rich. Maybe it's the money. Maybe my brain disease was somehow involved with money worries and the ensuing deceptions I practiced. I bet it was. But I am still deceiving Duke, still feel that I must. I can't stop now. Not yet. No deals, God, if that's what you have in mind.

Think how free I'll be if I'm really cured. I can go anywhere now. I can go to San Francisco, cross the Golden Gate! I haven't been to the city in months! I can go to museums by the hour now without having to drag a daughter along. Could it really be true that I'll no longer be assailed by those terrible fainting fits and fear of fainting fits: the whirling rooms, the sweating and trembling, the fiery flash of panic that's an electric shock treatment in itself? Oh, what a nightmare it's all been!

"Duke, Duke, I'm so happy."

"Huh?" he said sleepily.

"I'm just so happy. I can't say why, but I am."

He opened his arms to her, and slipping out of her clothes, she came into them. It was wonderful to be in a strange bed with Duke. He seemed more amorous, as if she were a strange woman; and she always responded more exuberantly, which was another good reason to go traveling together—all the different beds to inspire them.

The truth was that he rarely made love to her in their own bed anymore. She thought that this was due not so much to the omnipresent calculator as to his bad health and concomitant lack of good feeling. Obviously a man who didn't really feel good didn't feel sexy either. Nor did she find him as stirring to her own senses as she once had, but still, always after they did embrace, there was an afterglow, a reaffirmation of their enduring love for each other. And that, not pleasure, was the main thing, wasn't it?

Duke slipped off to dreamland again, and Augusta went out again to consciously test her return to sanity.

Ephraim walked in the Ormsby House door as Augusta walked out. Months later, when they came face to face, they would each have the feeling that they had seen each other somewhere before. The reason they exchanged looks at all was that redheads always notice each other, just as other minorities do. Redheads, deep down in their collective unconscious, know that they are a separate race, with their weird-colored hair and transparent or brown-spotted skin.

Augusta noticed that he had a complexion problem, as redheads often do, a sort of eczema condition that gave his cheeks a red, pachydermous look. And she noticed his chilling hauteur and his sensational body, but of course she had no way of knowing he was her killer-to-be.

What Ephraim noticed was Augusta's red hair and her nice, loose-limbed walk. He thought she was an unusual-looking woman. But he never dreamed as he passed her by that she would soon distinguish herself as the hardest hit of his career.

# 10

. . . . . *Ephraim Flawed*

EPHRAIM'S eczema had come suddenly upon him a week
ago. There seemed to be no earthly explanation for it.
He always enjoyed good health, had no allergies, and
was a rapid healer when injured. He had come to the
desert on the suggestion of a dermatologist who seemed
to feel the dry air might help. The eczema was on his
inner arms and behind his knees as well as on his
cheeks. It looked awful and and was maddeningly itchy.

The doctor also suggested that the affliction could be a
manifestation of some emotional upset. Ephraim could

78. . .

not tolerate this idea, since his emotions were always perfectly under control. Or they had been, up until ten days ago, when an extraordinary thing had happened, something he had determined not to think about. Now he figured he must examine it if it could have any connection with the hideous eczema.

Ephraim Johnstone came from Perry, Maine, the northeasternmost town in America, up by the Canadian border. His mother died in childbirth. His paternity was a mystery. He was raised by a grandmother who, even for a down-Mainer, was outstandingly taciturn—the ultimate mistress of pith, archenemy of jabber, with a bosom as granitic as Perry's coastal rocks. She could go weeks without saying boo. The boy Ephraim never knew caress.

So Ephraim grew up without developing any capacity within himself for giving or receiving affection, and he had no understanding of affection between other people. As he matured he nourished a bitter resentment of the parents who had deserted him and the starved environment he had been left to grow in.

It has been written that resenters, not haters, become the great assassins, because resentment is totally impersonal—directed not so much at anyone or anything as at the course of events of one's own life. Hatred allows for fierce emotion; resentment cauterizes emotion.

Raised as a solitary, Ephraim continued as a solitary —but he always enjoyed a vivid life of the mind. He was a child prodigy and was only fourteen when he went to the University of Vermont. This put the cap on his frightening solitude, for he was considered a freak, and being so much younger, he made no friends.

At eighteen, when he was drafted into the war in Vietnam, he had completed his college education. His first killing in combat moved him. He did not faint or vomit as many young men did, but he was shaken. Then, as all warriors can tell you, each killing got easier and easier. He did supremely well, and upon his discharge, he was tapped by a government-sanctioned organization for further training in the art of destroying human beings.

Now, sitting out on the pool terrace of the Ormsby House roof, his face to the sun, Ephraim thought about what had happened ten days ago when he had gone to Aikido of Tamalpais, entered the door, shed his shoes, and stepped to the mat.

There was an instructor there he had never seen before, wearing a *hakama*, the black skirt denoting achievement of the black belt.

Ephraim looked at the teacher and felt stunned. He felt his face grow warm as his mind formed the incredible thought, the impermissible thought: *this is my father.*

The man was exactly his height and build. They could have been twins from the neck down. He recognized the man's body as his own, even the hands, the large hands and the powerful wrists. The pigment of his skin was different, though—it was swarthy, not pale. And his hair was white. His eyes, like Ephraim's, were large and blue, intelligent, soft-seeing. His mouth was fuller, and it was . . . it was gentle. The teacher's whole aspect, although lofty like Ephraim's, was not arrogant. It was predominantly gentle.

The teacher sensed Ephraim's gaze and turned full towards it. He walked gracefully over to him. It was a lighter, looser walk than his own but very like it, disturbingly like it.

"Welcome," he said, and made the traditional Japanese bow, which Ephraim returned. "I've been waiting for you."

"What do you mean?"

"I've been putting all my intentionality on having a big man come to the *dojo* for me to work out with." He smiled.

The teacher obviously recognized that Ephraim, despite his white *gi* and white belt, was an accomplished martial artist who did not choose to flaunt his degree of advancement.

"Unfortunately," he continued, "this class is just ending, and our advanced class won't start for another hour. However, if you'd like to work out with me . . . ?"

"Good," said Ephraim.

"You would probably like to warm up. I have a few things to attend to."

Ephraim warmed up as the students left the mat, changed clothes, and left the *dojo*. The teacher did some business at the desk and, after five minutes or so, stepped onto the mat again. Again they bowed to each other. Then they began their dance. First the white-haired man was the attacker (*uke*), and Ephraim did the throws. Ephraim sent the lithe older man sailing through the air, saw how lightly he landed, rolled, and sprang to his feet. He could see what the teacher meant. It was very satisfying to work out with someone his own size. And, for a man in his fifties . . . The thought returned to Ephraim that the teacher was his father.

Ephraim eagerly took his turn as *uke*, following through on his attack, coming in at surprising angles, seeing how his opponent would respond, testing him. He was very good.

As the minutes went by, what had begun as a satisfying workout for the two tall men subtly changed and became a match. Ephraim was resolved to overcome this man and the thought he had about him.

Summoning all his speed and agility—striking, whirling, blending, with all his perfection—Ephraim attacked. They were alone on the blue mat in the big, empty, silent room where the sound of their breathing grew louder and harsher—loud, harsh breathing and sometimes a grunting sound or cry that seemed to come from the very centers of their being, from their genitals. They began to sweat so profusely that in their whirling motions the water flew from their faces like rain and sprinkled down onto the mat.

Ephraim wanted to get him. But . . . he couldn't! He could not touch him. Indeed, there were times when it seemed the teacher threw him down without touching him. The teacher was water, he was air. Now Ephraim didn't just want to overpower him. Now he thought to himself, I want to hurt him.

Again the dance changed: not a satisfying workout, not an exciting match of equals, but an old person defending himself against a young and vicious attacker. Ephraim became vicious. He began to use karate. But still the teacher wasn't there for him; he simply wasn't there. And then . . . then Ephraim flipped. He came at the teacher punching artlessly, flailing and punching like an angry, hurt little boy, hitting out with all his might, kicking, wanting so much to get him, to hurt him, to touch him.

And then . . . then the teacher embraced him. He wrapped his iron arms around Ephraim, holding him firmly and saying something to him, something . . . he had no memory of what. It was like a chanting, a soothing, a sound that dispelled the redness in his brain, stilled the wild trembling of his flesh that was the result of his exhaustion . . . and emotion.

He did not know how long the teacher held him in this way, how long it was until he regained his control. There was no time. When he stepped backwards out of the man's arms, when he stepped away from the embrace, backwards, and made himself look at the face, the teacher looked old, so old. He seemed to have aged exceedingly. To look at him was unbearable. His eyes . . . his eyes were so full and open that Ephraim felt he could fall into them.

Ephraim pulled himself together, even remembered to bow to the image of O Sensei before leaving the mat and to bow to the teacher, who also bowed. Then he turned, stepped off the mat, reached for his shoes, stepped through the doorway, and walked down the long iron stairway to the street.

Ephraim, under the Nevada sun, touched his cheeks. They were wet with tears. Tears? His fingers moved up to his eyes to see if the wetness really came from there. It did. What was this? Unbelievable. What was happening to him? He must be having a sort of . . . of . . . No, he wasn't going to give some crummy psychological explanation.

Disturbed, he got up and paced the terrace. He wiped the tears away with his sleeve. Whatever it was, he'd better not take a job until this weirdness was over. He'd made a vow when he entered the profession that in the event of his ever messing up a job, he'd quit. He was the best, and everyone in the industry, throughout the world, knew he was the best. He was held in awe.

But his reputation rested on his flawlessness, and just now he was feeling flawed, blemished. The eczema obviously signified some inner deficiency, some weakness. Ever since Fiji he'd felt something slipping, beginning to go. Then, in that *dojo*, he had lost control.

He left the terrace, took the elevator to his floor, entered his room. He went to the mirror and was amazed to see that his face was clear of the rash.

Well, that was quick work, he thought, feeling encouraged. Tomorrow I must strip down and sun my arms and legs too.

In the mirror, his reflection looked thoughtful, almost rueful. Or . . . or must I cry on them?

# 11

..... *A Mattress of Conscience*

MAY 15. Augusta's aunt's will was *ostensibly* in probate—that is, as far as Duke knew, it was still in probate. But it wasn't.

One day in March—a week before the international jogging idea in the market and three weeks before the weekend in Carson City—Augusta received seven brown envelopes addressed to Augusta Adams Gray, seven official-looking envelopes addressed to her own three names.

She took them to her half-room, which had been the

girls' bedroom before the garage and now contained a guest bed, a desk, and shelves full of Augusta's art books and other specially esteemed books. What with the shelves and desk and bed, there was no floor, really, no room to walk. But dormer windows on three of the four walls gave an airy feeling to the cramped space. Augusta spent much of her day in this room.

She slit the envelopes open with a silver letter opener. Each one contained a certificate, a large crisp piece of paper elaborately engraved, denoting a number of shares of a given stock in her own name. Augusta was very much struck that the brown envelopes had her name on them and the certificates did too.

Why, this is my money, she thought, amazed and impressed. It is not Duke's. It is not Duke's-and-mine. It is solely mine, for it is in my name alone. How interesting.

She went out to buy an afternoon paper, returned, hunted up the calculator, sat down at her desk with the securities, and after much difficulty (Duke could have told her instantly), apprised herself of her worth. Viz: 87 shares of Exxon at the asking price of $92 were valued at $8,004; 75 shares of General Motors at $63 were valued at $4,725; 250 shares of Pacific Power and Light at $21 came to $5,250; 300 St. Regis shares at $40 gave her a big $12,000; 200 Standard Oil Indiana at $43, $8,600; 150 Union Carbide at $70.65, $10,597; 100 Union Pacific at $78, $7,800. The total came to $56,976.

Bless my soul, said Augusta to herself. She put the securities back in their envelopes, put them under the mattress, and lay down on them to think.

She thought long and hard. Her mind was a carousel

of dreams and realities. As well, it was pushing and pulling in a serious struggle of conscience. She distrusted the stock market, but common sense and a lack of experience in handling large sums of money recommended leaving the money invested in this way. In all conscience she could not, however, for it was almost wholly invested in everything she most deplored, in companies whose philosophy she could not brook.

Exxon and Standard Oil continued to plunder and befoul the earth and to cheat the gas-buying public. They, along with Pacific Power and Light and others of their ilk, were using up energy and refusing to turn their faces to the sun—refusing to tap clean, pure, and inexhaustible solar energy. Union Carbide, ignoblest of all, was stripmining. General Motors? She could not forgive their unconcern for the air that gives us life. Possibly the paper mill, St. Regis, could escape the stigma of "Enemy of the Earth" if they grew their own trees. If so, she might keep it, along with the relatively harmless railroad.

After an hour, Augusta got off the mattress, having decided that she would not do anything hasty. She would think and plan and be as sensible and clever as she could be about this fortune bequeathed to her, which was in her name. That, in itself, was going to take some getting accustomed to.

By full moon in the middle of May, a month and a half after the writing of the first jogging route and almost two months after the receipt of the brown envelopes, life had altered for Augusta. She experienced only occasional twinges of phobia and could go about quite well by her-

self. Unfortunately, due to extended bus strikes in both
Marin County and the city of San Francisco, Duke had
to take the car to work every day, leaving Augusta with
no mobility to exercise her newfound freedom. But fortunately, she had her running and could run places.

By the middle of May, Augusta could run a fast pace
for thirty minutes at a stretch, a distance of three to four
miles. She ran to town to do her shopping and walked or
taxied back with the bundles. At first she was embarrassed to be seen running to and through town. People
would offer her lifts or stop their cars simply to ask her if
she was all right. Other people, walking or hanging out
around the square, made comments of a joking, rude,
contemptuous, or salacious nature.

But more and more, she dressed like a runner and
looked like a runner and didn't care what people thought
about her or yelled at her. There were other runners
around town, men (women seemed to keep to the track),
and they gave each other waves and smiles so that even
in the loneliness of running there was a feeling of being
one of a league, a band of people who understood each
other although they never spoke, who understood the
pain, discomfort, and total joy of running.

Better yet was running on the mountain trails, through
the primeval redwood forest, or out on the bare grassy
knolls high above the ocean, dodging deer and Anguses;
or down on the beach itself, running from the seaside
town of Stinson Beach to Bolinas, splashing through the
ebb and flow of waves, kicking up a glorious spray as she
ran.

She did flexibility exercises so that she grew supple as

well as strong and fleet. By May 15, although she was hurting almost all the time, Augusta glowed with health and strength.

In May the cherry tree was thick with leaves, and she looked up to see shiny cherries in various stages of ripening. A few were already hued the ultimate burgundy black, worth climbing the knobbly branches to take directly in the mouth and crush between tongue and palate for their exquisite, juicy sweetness.

Now, when Augusta lay down on the half-room mattress to think, her body weight pressed upon a new collection of papers. Of the seven securities, there were only two left, the two most innocent ones, with a combined value of almost twenty thousand dollars. This sum was for the girls' education. The dividends would be "plowed back in" so it could be allowed to "build," and Duke would be pleased. When he learned of it. But not yet. In due time she would explain to him that in all conscience she couldn't keep the other securities and support the enemies of the earth thereby.

Was she not, meanwhile, suffering some conscience pangs respecting Duke? Wasn't he more important to her than the earth? How did she feel when he called merrily from the bedroom, "Exxon is up seven points this week!" Or, "What a sweetheart that General Motors is; it just announced a fifty-cent dividend raise." How about some conscience pangs here?

No, no pangs. Some unhappiness, yes. She was loath to tell him they no longer owned these "sweethearts," to ruin his love affair by telling him that his houris, his beautiful dancing girls, dancing figures, were all creatures of his imagination—that these "paper gains" were even more illusory than that. They weren't being made on paper, but only on air. She hoped that when the time came to tell him the truth, the market would be taking a downward plunge. He would be despairing—then how overjoyed he'd be to hear that they had "bailed out" long ago when the market was high.

And she would tell him the truth. Soon. Soon all would be clear between them. Meanwhile, it was her money, and she believed she had done right about it. Under the mattress were the two paper securities she had kept. Also there were multiple packets of American Express travelers' checks worth eighteen thousand dollars. She considered this to be an advance from herself to herself for her International Jogging Book. This advance would allow Duke and her to take a year off for international travel when the time was ripe.

Ripe, Augusta? What is going to ripen the time? Or ripen Duke?

The fate of the remaining nineteen thousand or so was embodied in three pieces of paper. A white receipt represented four thousand dollars to pay off the remainder of the bank loan plus the penalty for paying it off—although why she should be penalized for cancelling her indebtedness was still a mystery to her—and a pink slip represented the thirty-two hundred dollars (including tax) she paid when secretly buying the Austin Healey.

The third piece of paper cost twelve thousand dollars, and Augusta was lying on that too. This paper, which was protected by glass because it was thin and old and very pretty, Augusta had wanted badly for several years. To explain, the story of Augusta and Ephraim must go back in time, not forward, but this will be the last backward glance. Then there will be no looking back for Augusta.

# 12

## . . . . . *Beloved Hiroshige*

FIVE years or so ago, when Augusta bought the three Hokusai woodcut prints, she engaged in further study of the *ukiyo-e:* pictures of the floating world. She read all she could. She met several gracious and helpful Japanese gentlemen who sold original woodcut prints and who loved to talk by the hour about the different artists. She pored through the Auchenbach collection of *ukiyo-e* prints at the Palace of the Legion of Honor Museum. She learned to tell an original from a copy, but that was not enough; she had to learn to tell a good early print

92. . .

from a later print or from a good early print that had faded. There were innumerable bad prints and an infinity of copies. In their day, the prints of the *ukiyo-e* were bought as cheaply as one might buy a postcard, and for the same reason—as a remembrance of the place where one had been. They were even used as wrapping paper, and many were thrown away as one would throw away postcards or wrapping paper. So nobody knew how many prints were left by any given artist or even how many had been originally printed.

After a hundred years, give or take, it seemed a good idea to start collecting these attractive pieces of paper, even to put some of them in museums, and during the thirties in Japan, one would pay twenty-five dollars for a print that had once cost pennies. In the fifties and six-ties, these same prints were going for as much as a hundred dollars. The masterpieces—for each prolific *ukiyo-e* artist had created masterpieces—were going for five hundred dollars! Now, in the seventies, the master-piece items were going for thousands. One did not need to be a financial genius to see that these prints were a good investment, but Augusta was not an investor; she was a lover, and when she studied these artists, she fell in love, not with Hokusai, but with Hiroshige.

Hiroshige, the painter of rain, the artist of the moon, the poet of travel. So strange that Augusta would come to love a man not of her time or of her land—a man most foreign. And yet, she knew him in all his moods: rollick-ing traveler, exuberant tale-teller, sad gentle poet, com-passionate friend, ambitious worker, consummate artist, God.

He worked so hard, traveled so much, and was so profoundly human. Yet, like the few great artists of the world, he had moments of godliness, and then, out of the hundreds of ordinary watercolor woodcut designs he painted, one masterpiece would emerge, a single picture so full of understanding and beauty that one came away ennobled. Out of the thousands of pictures painted by Hiroshige, there were perhaps a hundred superb ones, ten masterpieces.

It was thanks to her friendship with Hiroshige, her love for him, that Augusta learned to watch the cherry blossoms fall; to take long walks in the rain, to watch the shapes the trees took in it, to perceive the light that was cast by it and the way humans acted in it. Thanks to Hiroshige she noticed the mystery and splendor of the moon in all its phases, the line of the hills against the sky or against other hills, the motion of water, branches, grasses, petals, and people.

One picture is described thus in Muheshige Narazaki's book of Hiroshige's famous views: "Seba, the Thirty-second Station from the Sixty-nine Stations on the Kisokaido. Undoubtedly one of Hiroshige's finest works is this desolate landscape of a small moonlit river. Dropping, wind-blown willows are silhouetted against a large moon and dusky sky; thatched roofs peep over green paddies; and raftsmen pole their rafts through a world where a song would travel for miles on the night air. For whom do the reeds on the riverbank weep? To where does the frail vessel carry its load? These two figures would not exist without the river and moon: all is harmonious, elegant illusion."

Early in May, Augusta called a reliable art dealer in Larkspur and asked if this print was for sale anywhere. He replied, "It is coming up at auction in London. I already have a bid in for twelve thousand."

"I can't believe it's gotten so high. Just in the last year!"

"Everything has, Augusta. Do you want it?"

"Yes," she replied, her heart beating with excitement.

She got it. This harmonious and elegant illusion was hers. She had it framed in linen, cherry wood, and glass, then put it beneath the mattress. She was so happy to have it, yet she often found herself weeping over it. How terribly sad the landscape was, this landscape of Hiroshige's own soul that spoke to her of the death of his father when he was a boy and then of the death of his first bride, who had sold her kimono so that he might travel for a year and begin his artistic career. The river Styx, she thought, but the free-flowing river of life as well. Here is the pure world of one hundred fifty years ago, before industry, when the moon and sun lit the sky with a true color and a crystalline light that will never be seen from earth again.

How sad it is, she cried, believing that she wept for the spoiled earth or for Hiroshige, but not for herself.

But the more she ran, the more she got in touch with herself. Running cross-country, getting into distance, alone, there is no one to pretend to, least of all yourself, because you are beginning to respect yourself too much for that. After the first five or ten minutes comes the second breath, the release of the lungs and loosening of muscles, the lessening of labor. After almost an hour comes the mysterious third breath, the altered state when mind and body are unified and move effortlessly through time and space.

Now you know who you are, Augusta. And when, at the end of the run, you feel serene, is this God's doing? Is this God loving you? No. You did the running. It is you loving you. Are you lovable, Augusta?

Well, I could be, she thought. I wish I didn't have to sneak so, to be such a bamboozler.

Bamboozler? Isn't that putting too nice a name on it?

Well, yes. It has a larky ring to it that way. It's possible to admire a bamboozler, whereas a deceiver is a lower order of skunk. "What's in a name?" she quoted to herself. "That which we call a rose by any other name would smell as sweet."

Wouldn't a skunk, then, by another name raise an equal stink?

Augusta didn't answer yes to herself, but at least she asked the question.

# 13

. . . . . *Augusta*
*Disbosoms*

ONCE, when Augusta broached her enthusiasm for the
contemporary theory that marital partners should "talk
things out," Duke replied, "Communicating is quack-
ery." This impressed Augusta as a courageous statement
in the face of psychiatric authorities, ladies' magazines,
countless books on the subject, and the entire human po-
tential movement. As if talking with one another was
some sort of patent medicine, a trick, a placebo that he
was not going to be taken in by, not for one minute.

In truth, Duke found communicating in any depth

wearisome and unrewarding. He dealt with a difficult variety of individuals each day, worked very hard, was under a great deal of pressure most of the time, and the last thing he wanted to do when he came home was "communicate." He wanted to come home to a peaceful, clean house, a good meal, idle conversation, summary sex, and sleep, to renew himself for the next arduous but fascinating day. He retreated from intimacy, and when she pressed him for it, even begged for it, he retreated further.

Knowing full well that he did not encourage confidences from Augusta, Duke would nevertheless have been astonished at all the untold communications she contained within her bosom. She was brimming with messages that would interest him extremely. But he never dreamt it was so.

She lived such a simple life, it seemed to him, a simple, pleasant life in a little house that was easy to keep up, caring for two good girls who were no trouble to speak of. She had a nice group of women friends; she pursued her art studies, which gave her gratification—truly, he thought, her knowledge grew impressive over the years. He liked to hear her talk about her studies. He saw that her love of art added a necessary dimension to her life so that she did not feel confined to a daily humdrum. Yet it was an innocent pastime that did not intrude on the peaceful haven he required; his meals were always there for him, and she was too.

Every so often, every few years or so, she did come up with some crazy idea—like the jogging book. But because these ideas were always eccentric in the extreme, he was easily able to . . . not exactly discourage her, but show her the unfeasibility of it all so that after a short struggle, she would subside into her routine again.

One night toward the end of May, Augusta and Duke each lay on a segment of the L-shaped couch in front of a warm fire, and a false sense of intimacy arose that encouraged Augusta to try to "communicate" one more time.

It was a Friday night, and the girls were at a movie. Duke had begun to talk about the fifty thousand dollars from her aunt. She had steered him clear of those dangerous shoals, but now he was talking about the money that her mother had left to her brother. This was a subject that always fascinated him.

"By all rights your father should not have left his estate in the control of your mother, with her record of mental instability. He should have left it in trust for both of you with your mother getting the income for life."

"I know, but I think he felt it would insult her sanity to tie it up as if she were non compos mentis. And anyhow, Mummy wasn't insane really. Between breakdowns she was okay. Also, I suppose he realized that the money had to be available for huge sanitarium bills and for all the traveling she liked to do in between time."

"But aren't we talking about half a million dollars? More?"

"I guess."

"The income from that would have sufficed for the most extravagant single person."

"I suppose."

"You could have fought the will—your mother's, I mean."

"The will was as legal as could be." Augusta laughed.

"And we have been over this so many times. Mummy was deeply attached to my brother, and he to her. He looked after her through illness and wellness, whereas I practically never saw her from the time I fled to the West and married you. She had a right to leave it all to him if she chose. Poor Mummy. She had a perfect right to spend it all, too, if she wanted to, and not leave anything for anybody. It was her money, and Daddy obviously wanted her to think of it as hers. She could have done worse and left it to a gigolo, or done what my fabulously wealthy Uncle Ted did, which was to leave it all to a cat hospital."

"Surely the family fought that?"

"Perhaps they would have if it really was meant for the cats, but Uncle Ted was in love with the owner of the cat hospital, who was, alas, a man. In those days in New England one didn't want that sort of thing coming out. Better to forfeit the money."

"I still find it hard to believe that your mother was crazy. She was always so charming and intelligent when I saw her."

"I know. It's uncanny how she could put up a facade with other people. She could be a screaming frenzied maniac, and then an acquaintance would knock at the door. The next minute she would go to the door, smile, and say, 'How nice to see you.' All graciousness. In that minute she could even clear the whites of her eyes from the red that had filled them. But that was normal behavior. When she was really spiraling into a depression, she could not put up an effective pretense. But it is amazing how one can pretend to normalcy. May I tell you something about myself?"

"Of course."

Augusta got up and fiddled with the fire a moment. "I only tell you about it now that I'm okay." She glanced at him to see if he looked receptive. He did. He looked relaxed, even benign. His thick, spotless black hair was charmingly rumpled. It occurred to her that their only good conversations together seemed to turn on money, but if that could be a jumping off spot, all to the good.

"The fact is," she confessed, "I've been suffering for over a year from some sort of terrible phobia. It's hard to believe it, but I've been unable to go anywhere by myself for a long time. If I went alone I would grow so terrified, be so overcome with panic, that I would actually lose consciousness."

Seeing Duke's face, his frown, she faltered to a stop. All her fear of craziness returned, compounded by the fear of his knowing.

What a fool I am, she thought, to go to all that trouble of hiding it, only to tell him about it now.

But I want to tell. I don't want to hide. I want him to know.

But don't you see that he doesn't *want* to know.

She began speaking again, making light of it. "I can't imagine why this was. I don't think it was a symptom of a really deep problem, but rather some vagary, some wandering queerness that came to roost on me. I learned to live with it. I kept it from everyone. You didn't notice, did you?"

"No. But you say it's all gone now?" he asked.

"Yes. Knock on wood. It abandoned me in Carson City. When I got home I thought it might return, being back on familiar territory, but it hasn't. I'm so glad. You can't imagine the relief. Sometimes you don't know how awful something has been until it's over, and then you ask yourself how you ever managed."

"It's quite amazing that you did manage so well," he said reflectively. "I suppose one develops a certain amount of craft and wile in order to offset abnormalities and cope with life. Ideally we should get at the deeper problem that caused this, but that would probably take years of analysis and lots of money. . . ."

"But I just explained that it isn't a deeper problem. My mind is strong as a horse. And anyhow, I'm okay now. It's gone, probably roosting on some poor Nevadan —one of the casino owners, I hope."

"If it comes back—it or any other queerness, as you call it—you must tell me."

"I will. Oh yes, I will. I'd be happy to. How nice that you are interested." She felt a surge of warmth towards him.

Duke shot her a glance to see if she was being ironic, realized that she wasn't, and then felt touched. "Of course I'm interested. I care about you very much. You're my wife." But then Duke couldn't help feeling anxious and thinking, When Augusta gets her money from her aunt, I must see that it gets transferred to my name so that she doesn't do something crazy with it and deprive the girls. She will understand that I can best handle it for her. Actually, he thought, that money should be here this spring. If it doesn't come soon, I should make some inquiries to the executor of the estate.

Having decided that, Duke grew drowsy. He shut his eyes.

"You know, Duke, I wonder if I didn't run the phobia out of me, because its going coincided with my beginning to run."

"Sounds unlikely."

"Well, a friend was telling me the other day about a doctor down south who got to considering how man always used to run. It was natural for primitive people to run for a good part of each day. But civilized people are so inert. So this doctor encouraged twenty or so psychopaths and schizos to run an hour each day—an hour is a *lot* of running—and they did; he got them up to running about that much each day, and they all improved marvelously. Of course there's no question that if your body feels good, your mind is going to feel better too. Also, running makes you look better and eat better. Maybe the crazies started taking in more vitamins, which averted vitamin-deficiency-induced madness. But if you think that we are actually denying some deep primitive need by not running—maybe as serious a denial as not having sex, not procreating—who knows? Who knows? It opens a whole world of conjecture, don't you think, Duke? Duke?"

Duke was asleep. Just as well. Augusta was in full conversational flow now. She might have got carried away and unbosomed herself more. Jogging would have led to the book, the book to her inheritance, and thence ineluctably to the traveler's checks. She mustn't be hasty.

I mustn't be hasty, she reminded herself. The time is still not ripe. She repeated these two phrases. Then she looked at Duke sleeping and felt despair. How can the time ever be ripe? It is beyond ripeness now; it is rotten.

# 14

## . . . . . *Four Masks*

MAHLER was on the stereo this last day of May. Through the view windows, the bay looked almost painfully blue next to the gold hills, some of which were partially blackened by grass fires.

Against the white walls were four masks, supernatural totems which possessed the wearer, bestowing the power of a dead spirit or of a demon. The masks were not intended to be beautiful. Feeling and religious relevance were what mattered to the artists who had made them. Yet the creation of these masks was subtle and profound,

*104. . .*

the execution skillful. This art, although called primitive, was as elegant and mysterious as the culture it served.

One mask, over the fireplace, was from the Sepik River district of New Guinea. It was made of wood, painted red, white, and black in a curved style—no straight lines, only circles and arcs. This mask represented a demon or an ancestor.

The skull mask over the desk came from the Guamantuna tribe of New Britain. It was a painted human skull with soft parts modeled in resin. This mask probably had to do with a death cult.

On the wall over the couch was a simple wood mask from the Mortlock Islands which portrayed a benevolent spirit.

The fourth mask leaned against the wall beneath the third. It had the same restrained power as the other masks but conveyed little or no expression, was less vivid. The heavy eyelids were almost closed beneath the arcs of brows. The nose was a straight line, as was the mouth. The mask was made of pale, live human skin. The lips were full, and one could imagine them smiling and sensual if the wearer were possessed by a different sort of demon—if the wearer hadn't so very much to do with death.

Ephraim was thinking about "his father."

Time after time he had made himself think about and reenvision the scene at the *dojo.* He did not block it out. He decided to get into it and through it. He was used to listening to his body and his mind; now he would tune in to his emotions (which apparently did exist, after all).

He understood that he was a repressed, inhibited person, understood this fact and accepted it, and chose to be this way. He believed that it set him apart, made him unique—a purely physical and intellectual man, unblemished by emotion or by attachment. Perfect.

So he had gone over and over the scene with his father until he was no longer moved by it at all, realizing in this instance that to repress the memory would be to give it power.

Now he was determined to get a contract and prove he was as good as ever. Any job would do. He would not be particular this time. Also, he needed money badly. His bank balance could sustain his life-style for about one more month. The trouble with his profession was that he couldn't seek out a client; they had to come looking for him.

He had just finished cleaning his favorite gun, the one he had designed himself—a weapon as Byzantine as his novels, so clever and convoluted that a stupid assassin, or an assassin with reactions less hair-trigger than its trigger, would end by killing himself with it.

The gun lay on the coffee table in front of him, and Ephraim relaxed on the couch, listening to Mahler, ready to perform with perfect professionalism some murder. Soon. He was like a runner who had peaked in his training, but had no race to run.

The three other masks, intended for faces, not walls, looked impotently down on him.

# 15

## . . . . . *The Second International Jogging Route*

VAL went through the little gate and hailed her sister in the cherry tree. "You should wait until the cherries are riper; you're picking them much too soon."

"If I don't get them," Lee called down, "the birds will. And all the neighbor kids. And Mom."

"Where is Mom? Is she home?"

"No, she's on one of her runarounds."

"She's hardly ever home these days." Val threw her library books on the lawn and climbed the ladder that Lee had set under the huge old tree. "I admire her running, though. I didn't think she'd really stick to it."

"She *has* to run. Dad takes the car every day."

"I think she secretly bought the Austin Healey."

"She did?" asked Lee, very excited. "Why didn't she tell us?"

"Well, I think she doesn't want Dad to know. You know how he is about money."

"Poor Mom. But where is the car? How do you know?"

"I've seen her in it a couple of times. She wears a really pathetic disguise so she won't be recognized—a scarf and dark glasses. Next time I see her I'm going to wave and shout, 'Hi Mom!' "

"I don't think she should keep it a secret from *us*! Then we don't get to ride in it. It's not fair."

"But it is nice that she can go places alone now," Val said.

"What do you mean?"

"Well, seems like she could never go anywhere by herself. She always had to take one of us along, or one of the old people around here. She'd pretend she was doing them a favor, but she really just wanted someone to come along with her."

"Hey, that's right! I never noticed. How come?"

"Search me. It's just like you never used to like spending the night at anyone's house. You'd cry if you got invited somewhere." Val laughed.

Lee tried to think of some peculiarity in which Val indulged, but she couldn't come up with one. They were both quiet, eating cherries, spitting out pits.

"Is Dad here?" Val asked.

"No, he's gone to Bangkok." Lee looked sad as she

said this. She loved her father very much and missed him when he went away.

"I've decided for sure to graduate this year," Val confided. "I want to get out into the world. I'm so bored."

"Will you go to Princeton?"

"If I can get in."

"It will be so long until I'm a famous ballerina and can go dancing around the world. Mom just has to run a little while before she's ready to go running around the world. Dancing takes so long to learn."

"Long is right. Maybe never. You're trying to be the hardest thing there is to be, you know. It's worse than learning an instrument, because your whole body is your instrument, and it's human."

"That's okay," said Lee with a sudden surge of belief in herself. "It just takes practice."

Meanwhile, Augusta—in her "pathetic disguise"—was roaring up the Waldo Grade in the blue sports car, feeling very low to the ground and exposed to the elements as contrasted to being in the bulwark of the Mercedes. She had the feeling that cars in front of her didn't even see her in their rearviews, and she was right.

But she wasn't frightened. She was exultant. As she crossed the Golden Gate Bridge, she sang at the top of her lungs, which for Augusta meant the emission of a thin, quavery, and horribly off-tune sound—a poor spider web of a singing voice that she only let loose when no one could hear it and make fun.

She took joy in crossing the bridge, in the day which had been swept crystal clear by a north wind, in the wisps of song that were carried away by the private breeze of her darling, darling car—her car that handled like a dream, responded to fingertips rather than arm wrenches, bounded forward at the very thought of acceleration so that she scarcely needed to press down her foot.

She was happy, too, because Duke had gone off on a business trip. It was as if a manhole cover had been lifted from her back, and she admitted this feeling to herself. And he was happy to go. He loved his trips. Which was one reason why she had thought he'd want to do the jogging book with her, why she had believed it would make him a happier man and theirs a happier marriage.

Now she was off to do her Second International Jogging Route in San Francisco, the most beautiful city in the world to her knowledge, second only to Rio in Duke's opinion.

She had heard of a route that was part of America's newest national park, the Golden Gate National Recreation Area. It started at the St. Francis Yacht Club and ran along the edge of the bay to the bridge. It sounded appropriate for her book and would involve no turns at all, or street names or trees, and certainly no churches.

Was she just going through the motions now, or did she still hope to do the book? Could she do it alone?

I don't know, she answered herself, for more and more she was answering as well as asking. In the meantime, I love the running for itself.

Like Lee, she was coming to understand the value of practice, the art of practice, of effort which brings grace.

Practice forced her on, to go farther, to go faster. Just when she felt she'd reached the limit of her physiology, she found herself on a new plateau of possibility. Every push beyond her limit in fact increased her capacity, was another step up to a higher plateau, and changed not just her running but her life.

She parked in the Yacht Club parking lot and stood for a while on the beach watching a fisherman and observing the traffic on the bay: a freighter, low in the water, heading out; the ferry boat ploughing across from Sausalito; a fishing boat; and one solitary sailboat, a dancer among the briny marchers. Bewitched by these nautical comings and goings, by the solemn fisherman, she turned and began to run along the trail, oblivious of the route, her mind empty, in a suspended state.

She maintained this state of mind for about a mile and a half until her consciousness was aroused by the impending bridge and a vista of it never seen before—the monstrous filigree of ironwork that was its underbelly. In the distance, she also perceived a male runner coming towards her, right towards her, not veering at all. And when she veered to avoid collision, he veered to collide. He caught her in his arms.

"Augusta!"

"Daniel!"

She stepped back and looked at him with pleasure. "So this is what is meant by 'running into an old friend.' "

He laughed. "Come on and run my way and tell me what you've been up to. It's almost time for you to turn around anyhow."

"No, no . . . please come with me to the bridge. I

want to touch the Golden Gate Bridge at its roots; I'll
tell you why afterwards."

They ran out onto the point where the roar of the
waves below merged with the very similar sound of
bridge traffic above. Augusta touched the great cement
pier, felt true awe, then turned to begin the return trip.

They set off at an easy pace, talking together. This was
a new experience for Augusta, running and talking, and
her body moved effortlessly along, her senses now open
to everything: the path, the bouquet of buildings in the
distance that was the city of San Francisco, her companion.

She had known Daniel Swanson when she lived in the
city. They had played tennis at the same public court,
and she would see him there on the mornings when he
was ashore, for he was an officer on a freighter that plied
the South Seas. He was always pleasant and cheerful
and, unlike most men who played well, never loath to
play with a woman. He was a bachelor but not a pre-
dator, an easygoing, diffident, good-humored person—
not handsome but sensual-looking, someone who obviously enjoyed life without making a fuss about it.

They ran along and chatted together, both saying how
much easier it was to run than to try to get a court these
days, although it didn't allow for much camaraderie—but
wasn't it pleasing just to run and talk like this. People
should run together as well as alone, although they
agreed it would have to be just the right person to make
the running seem as effortless as this was. Augusta told
him about her International Jogging Book, and he said,
"Good idea!" in a way that warmed her and "Wonderful
idea!" in a way that made her love him.

She told him more about the book, and then he told her that he had his captain's papers now but that he was first mate on his current vessel. The "old man," as he called the captain, was a good sort, and Daniel didn't mind taking orders as well as giving them—he was in no hurry to command a ship. Then Augusta told how she lived in Mill Valley now and what a nice town it was, how her daughters were growing and that there were cherries on the tree. Too soon they were back at the Yacht Club.

Augusta mopped her face and felt the sweat trickling between her breasts and down her ribs. She experienced the lovely light-headedness that a good run engendered.

"Do you live here in the marina, Daniel?"

"No, I'm up on Telegraph Hill."

"That's right. I remember. With a view of the piers so you can see when your ship's in."

"Yes, but I ship out of Oakland now."

"Maybe we could get some sandwiches at a deli and have some lunch here on the Marina Green," Augusta suggested, not wanting to relinquish him, entranced by the running with him, feeling affectionate.

"Well, I think I'd like to get home and shower and . . ." and . . . "

"Perhaps I could come," she said boldly, being so light-headed and happy. "I could fix us a sandwich there and see your view!"

"Why, sure. Fine idea. Do you want to follow me in your car?"

"Yes, I do. I will." She got in her dashing little car, followed his staid-looking Peugeot to North Beach, and parked as near to his apartment on the hill as possible.

At the hilltop where Vallejo Street ended and became a staircase going down the other side, there stood a glamorous new apartment building of redwood and glass. Daniel lived next to this in a shabby gray stucco building three stories high. They walked up two flights and entered a small penthouse, a forecastle consisting of living room, bath, kitchenette, and tiny bedroom. The large window allowed a mellow light into the cool, still interior, as well as framing a view of the East Bay and the clear blue spring sky.

While Daniel went right to his shower, Augusta made sandwiches. She rummaged and found one tomato, some mustard and mayonnaise, and green onions, all of which enhanced the synthetic bread and packaged bologna. She felt completely at home, as if creating sandwiches in a bachelor's pad was a common occurrence for her. As her high from the run subsided, however, she did pause to ask herself what on earth she thought she was doing here.

Dan came out of the bathroom combing back his wet hair, a towel wrapped around his waist, and she saw that he had a surprisingly unmuscular-looking body for one so athletic. But he was well formed, light-footed, graceful.

"It's all yours."

Augusta blushed. "What is?"

"The shower. Go ahead. I'll open some wine to have with these scrumptious sandwiches."

"Well, I . . . I . . . "

"Go on. Go ahead," he said encouragingly, and laughing, he pushed her towards the bathroom.

So she went and showered.

"There's a clean robe on the door," he called after her.

Augusta showered and tottered out a few more whispers of song under the noise of the water. She dried herself off, felt great, put on the robe, and went back out. She couldn't remember when she'd had so much fun.

He was still in the towel, and his hair was wet and slicked back, but the dark blond curls were springing forward, here and there lopping over his forehead as they dried. Then she knew she wanted to embrace him. "Will you kiss me?" she asked shyly.

His face lit up enchantingly. "Happy to," he said. He did kiss her, and it was very nice for them both. He kissed her and did some other things too, without her asking. Then he looked at her and inquired gently, "Have you had a lover since you've been married?"

She had not. Nor had she had a lover before she was married. But with wonderful presence of mind she lied and said yes, and so he led her to his bed.

At least an hour went by before they got around to the sandwiches, which they ate with a fine, cool wine. Then it was back to bed, and a couple of hours more went by. Augusta just didn't believe that you could spend so much time making love or that there were so many different physical, tactile ways to express feelings. She was astonished at how incredibly sweet and pleasing it all was and how she could lose herself in a way she never had before—except, she thought curiously, for the times when I was having natural childbirth.

He came to her body like a gardener to a garden, taking as much pleasure in the shy wildflower as in the flamboyant rose. And such juiciness, such nectar flowed from her that she was amazed it was from herself and not from him. She put her fingers to the place to see if the wetness really came from there. It did. How wonderful!

No, the nectar was not from him, for he was long in loving, wonderfully long, and when he did finally come among her many comings, it was as if the gardener had orchestrated a sudden simultaneous flowering from bud to bloom, the blossoms manifesting their emergence with sound as well as scent, the gardener responding with gratified groans of pleasure and relief.

"The sound of flowers blooming," Augusta sighed.

"What's this?"

"Nothing. I was just feeling like a garden."

"Good. And I'm the mole, tunneling, burrowing, humping."

She laughed.

This Dan was such a tender, thoughtful, cozy, huggable man; he made love to her as though there was nothing in life he enjoyed so much. She noticed that he ate his sandwich with great gusto too, and that when he drank his wine he stretched his lips out for the sip, simianlike, and swirled it around on his tongue and actually smacked his lips with the pleasure of it. It was a lot like the way he kissed her nipples.

Augusta was just wide-eyed with the wonder of it all, and she lay langorously in the little bedroom that, for a seagoing man, was only moderately shipshape. The mattress was firm and bouncy, the sheets were rainbow-patterned, covered over with a wonderfully soft delft blue blanket. She was just thinking that she'd never go home when he asked her when she would be expected back; it was five o'clock.

"Five o'clock. Oh, my goodness."

They showered together, another new experience for Augusta, and then they dressed. Augusta wished she had something fresh and pretty to put on and noticed that Dan was dressing in a suit and tie. Where was he going? With whom? Indeed, he had two whole lives she didn't know about, one on land, and another at sea.

He dressed and groomed himself briskly and efficiently, moving into high gear, and Augusta, once back in her sweat suit, found that she was sitting and watching him as he moved around the little apartment and that she was wondering about him.

He noticed her doing this and looked surprised, maybe surprised to find that she was still there. "Well, lady," he said, helping her to her feet and walking to the door.

"Are you going out for the evening, Daniel?"

"Yes, I'm going to dinner with some friends."

"Oh." He had not said when they would meet again. She waited for him to say. Then, "When shall we meet again?" she asked. "Do you want to see me again?"

"Of course," he responded gallantly.

"Oh, good! Tomorrow? Or the next day?"

"Not unless you're an awfully good swimmer."

"But . . .what do you mean?"

"I'll be at sea."

"Oh, no!"

"Yes."

"Then we can't see each other for awhile."

"That is correct. Not for five weeks, in fact."

"Oh, no!"

"That's how long it will take me to get to Australia and back."

"That's so long," Augusta said woefully, her heart heavy with dismay. Then she smiled a little. "At least you'll be safe from earthquakes. Isn't a ship the safest place to be?"

When he looked bewildered at this unexpected turn in her conversation, she grew excited and said, "No one has noticed but me. I mean, no one has really counted. In the last six weeks alone there have been seven earthquakes in the world, four of them major. This appears to be the deadliest quake year we've had in ages, maybe since the beginning of time. Think of Guatemala! Panama! Italy! Russia! Russia naturally didn't mention hers at first for fear it might be misconstrued as a misplaced hydrogen explosion . . . "

Daniel was holding open the door.

"But imagine! What does it mean? Is this God speaking?"

Daniel patted her gently on the back, sort of pushing her towards the door.

"As for our drought! At sea, too, you will be safe from California burning. Fortunately for us, being on the coast, we can convert seawater for drinking, but the seawater won't reach to quench the fires in the hills and mountains. It's really scary. Poor Daniel; you look so quizzical. It's just that I'm so sad to leave you. Whenever I'm sad I talk a lot . . . and stupidly. I'm sad that I won't see you for so long. Thank you. Thank you for the very nice time."

"Thank *you*," he said, smiling.

They embraced a final time. Augusta looked at him to see if he seemed at all grief-stricken to part with her, but either he was a first-class masker of emotions or he didn't feel anything. The putting on of his suit seemed to signify something. His dressing for dinner had estranged them. "Could you write to me while you're gone?" she asked timidly.

"No."

"No? A postcard?"

"You are a married woman, Augusta."

"I always get the mail."

"I'm sorry," he said. "But I'll see you in five weeks."

Augusta started down the stairs, then turned back. "Could I write to you?"

"Yes, if you want to. Sure!" He gave her an address where the mail would be forwarded to him.

Then they parted a final time.

Augusta drove home in a daze.

What have you done? she asked herself.

Uh . . . nothing.

Not nothing. Something. Something bad.

Oh.

You, who have never done anything worse than build two bedrooms behind your husband's back, have now deceived him in earnest.

Bamboozled?

No, deceived.

But I *love* Daniel.

Love? Well, it is not Hiroshige you have fallen in love with this time, not Hiroshige at all.

Now, just a minute. Dan is quite a lot like Hiroshige. He is a gentle person, a traveler, a tale-teller. He must have a lot of poetry in his soul to love the sea as he does. And he doesn't like unpleasantness. Remember what a termagant Hiroshige's second wife often was? When she got into one of her contentious periods, Hiroshige would just leave home for a few days, quietly go out the door, probably with his paper and paints well in hand. I can imagine Dan doing exactly that, only he is ahead of the game for never having married at all.

You and Hiroshige didn't fuck.

This is true.

You are Duke's wife.

Very well, that's true too, but I'm not a piece of goods. At one point Dan spoke of me as being "someone else's property." Ugh! Something has been revealed to me this day, which is: *my body is my own.* It's as free as my mind. Duke can't forbid me to make love with it any more than he can forbid me to run with it.

That sounds pretty thin.

I am my own person, answerable only to myself. I am just as free to love Dan as I am to love Hiroshige and Duke.

Don't you feel guilty?

I feel . . . wonderful. I feel so glad about my body! I feel scared too, scared of myself. . . .

And of Duke? What if he found out?

I'd be more scared. I pray he doesn't. He mustn't.

Then leave it alone. You've had this nice day. Don't see Daniel again.

No, I have to. I want to. I will.

There is no talking to you, Augusta. You will just have to live and learn. Or die and learn.

# PART TWO

# 1

## . . . . . *Augusta Gray, Runner*

FIVE weeks passed for Augusta. The drought worsened, but California burned only somewhat. Sprinklers were banned, lawns turned gold and then brown. A reverse snobbism held sway. To have a trim green lawn was despicable. Likewise a washed car. And water in toilet bowls must be yellow to show you only flushed "number two."

Val went east for a month to visit cousins and uncles and aunts and Princeton. Lee absorbed herself in a summer ballet program. Duke returned from the Orient.

He worked hard. When he was home, he fixed Augusta with a jaundiced eye. She now ran an hour a day, seven to eight miles at a stretch. She had taken up with other running people, strange people—really odd—and talked about entering races. One day she was ecstatic because a friend had timed her on the mile and she'd run it in six forty-six. A month later she ran it again, determined to break six and a half, and she did: six twelve. For a woman well into her thirties, who had only just started to run, that was fast indeed, she thought. And she was right. Duke thought it was fast too, but what was the point of running fast—or of running at all at her age?

In conversation, Augusta was only animated when talking about running. She had become a running bore. Instead of reading about art, she read about running. She constantly quoted people he had never heard of: Dr. Sheehan, Mike Spino, George Leonard, and Michael Murphy.

She did her flexibility exercises on the front lawn for all the world to see and sometimes meditated there as well—which to "all the world" looked even stranger. Only a three-year-old neighbor boy thought it seemed perfectly natural. He earnestly imitated her every move as best he could. Then, standing on the picket fence, he waved her off as she went running down the street.

She had stopped wearing makeup, as it didn't mix well with sweat. Instead of wearing her hair up, she let it fly. She found that a bra chafed her when she ran, so she ceased wearing one even when she wasn't running— Augusta, who had always been modest, and whose nipples were well defined! But nipples weren't all that showed beneath her clothes; bones did as well. All in all, Duke thought Augusta was looking awful.

"That's okay. Dr. Sheehan says that if a friend tells him he's looking well, he knows he needs to lose five pounds."

"I don't give a shit what Dr. Sheehan says or how he looks. I do care about your looks. You have always had such beautiful legs; now they're becoming horribly muscled."

This hit her where it hurt, for her legs had always been what she liked best about her external self. "I don't think that's true, Duke. Men's legs get muscled up from running, but women's really don't. I think they look better now. I've lost all that flab I was getting on my thighs. Anyhow, I really don't care. Isn't it better for the whole body to feel so great, so healthy and strong, than to have beautiful legs?"

"You will never again have those fantastic legs," he said, almost mournfully.

"If only you would run, too. Won't you please come out with me and try a little bit of running? You will be so surprised at . . . "

"No!"

What of her jogging book, her marital and physical odyssey? In the face of all this negativism, did she, could she, still intend to do it and to persuade Duke to join her? Yes, she knew more certainly than ever that she would do it. As for Duke . . . it had been her idea to ease him into a running schedule and get him hooked on it before producing her final plan and her "advance monies," but . . . well, wouldn't it be wonderful to do it with Daniel instead? Daniel, who already *did* run, who loved to travel, who was so congenial! Of course, they'd only been together that one time, but she thought they would make fine companions over a long range. Truly it was a jubilant notion!

If that is the case, Augusta, shouldn't you tell Duke about the money?

Yes, I really should. I should.

On the appointed day, July 7, Augusta was out on the Marin Headlands sighting Daniel's returning ship.

"Ship ahoy!" she shouted for the joy of it. When she had watched it ply from the horizon to the bay, passing beneath the bridge, she returned home and sat waiting by the phone for his call. At last, the five weeks had passed.

# 2

*. . . . . Daniel at Home*

DANIEL unlocked the door of his penthouse and walked in. He put down his suitcase and threw his duffel bag of dirty laundry on the closet floor, flicking on the television in the same motion. He missed television when he was at sea, especially the news; but after three days on land it always lost its charm, especially the news.

There was a fine layer of dust over everything, but a quick vacuuming would take care of that. He always left it clean and orderly when he shipped out. He turned on the refrigerator, put in some ice trays, then opened his suitcase to get out one of the blue and gray jugs of Glen Garry—the best Scotch in the world—which he could only get in New Zealand. He was glad to see that holes hadn't been burned in his clothes by the packet of passionate letters from Augusta. He glanced at the pile of mail he had found in his box. Probably there were more letters from Augusta there. He sighed. What was he to do about Augusta?

He had always made it a rule not to fool around with married women. What was the point when there were so many unmarried ones? Also, her husband was associated with the shipping industry and was a powerful figure. Daniel had seen Duke more than once. A very tough character, Dan decided, in the way that those Ivy League types can sometimes look, though not in the macho cigar-chomping way of the Mafia or the union boys. It was something in the eyes, probably intelligence, which was why they didn't need to show muscle. Horrible dressers too, those Ivy Leaguers, in their soft saggy suits that always looked slept in (Duke did, in fact, sleep in his suits). And they never went in for jewels or any kind of flash (Duke wore a Timex). That was what was so obnoxious—the feeling that they didn't need to, that everyone would know they were rich and well born just by the way they carried themselves and by the look in their eyes, a kind of superconfidence it all added up to, he guessed.

Daniel went to the bedroom and made up his bed, pursuing his thoughts regarding Augusta Gray.

No, you were just asking for needless trouble to mess with a married woman—but there she was that day, looking so forlorn because their run was over and he was going to leave her. When she actually invited herself over, what could he say? And when she asked him to kiss her, what was a gentleman and sportsman to do but oblige the lady? And if ever a lady was hungry for love, it was Augusta. But she gave as much as she got, and he had to admit he had thought of her more than once while lying in his bunk of a night, or morning, depending on the watch.

He remembered her on the very bed he was making now. What a lovely body she had, a combination of fragility and power unique in his experience.

Daniel sighed again. And now she had written him all these letters. How could he let her down and not call?

The bed made, he went to check the ice. It was ready enough. He poured the Glen Garry over a glass of it and sat down in front of the telly, where he became totally absorbed in the news: a forest fire, a strike, the drought, the stock market (up), sports, and weather.

Yes, weather. He lost his absorption and thought again of Augusta. There was also a dippy quality about her that made him uneasy. She wasn't like other women he had known and on whom he could depend to act in an expectable way. That earthquake business, for instance. According to her letters, there had been two more in China, and the Teton River Dam had burst and flooded twenty-five miles of towns and farms, possibly because of a temblor. Not that Augusta was causing these quakes—he laughed to himself—but what other women did he know who counted earthquakes or, for that matter, who ran?

Women her age didn't run; they married or divorced or drank. They pursued a career or men or pleasure. They swam, sunbathed, played tennis, raised children badly. They traveled and took pictures and talked. God, how they talked! He did not know one other woman who ran.

He looked at his watch. It was too late to call her now; her husband would be home. He felt something akin to regret and looked at the phone unhappily. Then it rang. He reached over for it. Maybe it was Augusta.

"Hello? Well, hello, lady, how's things? Where are you calling from? Here in San Francisco, eh? Very good. Well, what's doing? Shall we have dinner? I'm just in. Good. I suppose you're at the Fairmont. Okay, I'll be there in . . . forty-five. Ta-ta."

Dan showered, then dressed leisurely and impeccably. He selected a brown suit from his vast wardrobe, a light brown shirt (dark brown monogram on the right cuff), and a tie of brown, green, and white paisley design. All his suits and shirts were personally tailored. He looked in the long mirror and gave a smile of approval, then remembered to don the watch and ring she had designed for him and had made up in gold and precious jewels. The two items—he'd had them appraised—were worth a small fortune. It would not do to appear without them, would not do at all. Luckily he'd remembered at the last minute to take them from the ship's safe and stick them in his bag.

Daniel had a last small slosh of Glen Garry, turned off the TV, and looked around. He was feeling increasingly apprehensive about Augusta's letters. He'd better destroy them. He tore them up and placed them on the grate of the Swedish fireplace he'd installed last winter. He watched them burn, pulverized the ashes, then departed for the Fairmont to meet Evalyn. Goodbye, Augusta.

# 3

##### ..... *Three Conversations*

. . . 1

EVALYN woke up the next morning in the familiar comfort of her usual suite at the Fairmont Hotel: the diplomat suite on the twenty-third floor of the tower. Like her Sacramento house, it was furnished in brown and beige, except that the carpeting was in a leopard pattern— something she would never dare to purchase for her house, but which the racier side of her nature was delighted to rent by the day.

A pretty high price to pay for the fun of padding around on spots, she thought, but then there's the view.

She got out of the oval-shaped bed and pulled the drapes in both the bedroom and the living room. The view swept from bridge to bridge, from Golden Gate to Oakland Bay. A fabulous white summer fog was billowing in the Gate and rolling around the islands and peninsulas of the bay like a cloud that had fallen from the blue sky for a lark, curious to have a feel of the water.

Good show, she thought, but it's really the rug and the spaciousness and the handy location that encourages me to pay five hundred and fifty dollars a day for this. No, untrue. It's the view that people gasp at, and I like people to gasp. I suppose I pay to get the gasps. Maybe that's why, deep down, I really like the shape of Nancy, because people gasp. Although Daniel scarcely gave either Nancy or the view a nod.

She went back to bed and thought about Daniel. Slowly she went over in her mind the evening she had spent with him, every word and gesture—from the greetings at the beginning to the lovemaking at the end, bracketing the sumptuous dinner at Trader Vic in between. They were both devoted to good food, so there hadn't been a lot of talk during dinner.

Room service knocked politely and wheeled in her breakfast: squeezed grapefruit juice, croissants, honey and butter, a silver pot of coffee. She ate slowly and thoughtfully, sipped her coffee, then rang up Nancy in the suite's adjoining bedroom and asked her to come by for a chat.

Nancy arrived presently. Evalyn thought she had a

light, springy step for such a fat woman, as if the last thing a fattening body forgot was the walk of its original self. Evalyn couldn't imagine anyone letting herself get so gross. And Nancy had been so pretty.

"It isn't good for you, this extra load you carry," she said, thinking aloud to her friend. "It is just as if you were walking around carrying fifty-pound suitcases in each hand everywhere you go."

Nancy smiled. "Only imagine how I feel when I *am* carrying suitcases." She sat down on Evalyn's bed.

"You will die, you know, if you don't start dieting in earnest."

"Yes, I suppose I will. Death is nature's way of telling us to slow down."

"You have your subtle ways of trying to make me feel this fatness of yours is somehow my fault. However, it is my contention that you would have grown fat in any case, no matter what path you chose. You are a neurotic."

"Right. I'm neurotic as all hell."

"I did not make you neurotic, although I may have increased your nervousness about life. I know I am not easy to live with, but who is? I take no blame, Nancy. You are responsible for yourself. You are your own authority. Anyhow, I am incapable of guilt feelings."

"I know. You're very lucky."

"Guilt is useless. Guilt is the glory of the devil. It causes more harm in the world than anything else."

"That's an interesting theory."

Evalyn threw back her covers and got up to pace the large room. "Well, I didn't ask you in here to theorize. I want to talk to you about Daniel. How did he seem last night when you saw him?"

"Just the same. He is always the same, always so pleasant and congenial. He's such a nice person. He seemed glad as ever to see you, although he's not a man who shows much emotion." Nancy helped herself to Evalyn's second croissant, with a great gob of honey and butter. "I don't mean that he's in the least a cold person; I mean he has cool, he's unflappable. He would never be carried away by either anger or joy, which is not to say he isn't perfectly capable of feeling both."

"No one feels joy, Nancy. Except, perhaps, some saints and a few little children."

Nancy thought this was an interesting thing for Evalyn to say. It was surprises like this that kept her fascinated by the woman, that kept her Evalyn's factotum, and that inspired her devotion.

Evalyn lit one of her occasional cigarettes and fit it into a jade and ivory holder. "It's my opinion that Daniel has someone else."

"How could he? He was with you during his entire last leave, in Acapulco. He only returned here for one day and one night before sailing. Since then he has been at sea."

"He met *me* at sea."

"Granted, but don't forget, you screened all the passengers on this last sailing and there wasn't a woman under fifty-five."

"There is someone. I trust my intuition. There is someone he cares about, and I am going to find out who it is."

"And then?"

"Destroy her, of course."

Of course, thought Nancy. How silly of me to even ask. Evalyn would act directly upon a jealous impulse that would only pass like a dark shadow through a normal person's mind.

"Call this number, Nancy. A Mr. Johnstone. Ask him if he will please meet with me here this morning. Be sure to tell him it's business. He has a horror of anything that smacks of pleasure."

### . . . 2

I am a fool, a goose, and an ass, said Augusta to herself, sitting woefully in her half-room on that same morning when Evalyn was talking to Nancy. Here I am like a fifteen-year-old, hanging by the phone. Obviously he isn't going to call. He's had all yesterday afternoon, last night, and this morning, and he hasn't called and he isn't going to.

Live and learn.

No, nuts to living and learning. I don't want to learn. I want to make love to Daniel. I don't want to learn anything about living; I want to live! And love! And run! I haven't even run for twenty-four hours because of hanging around this stupid phone.

Well, why don't you call him? What's this rule that the woman doesn't call? Who made that rule? That rule went out years ago. Call him, why don't you? Go ahead.

All right. All right, I will. I'll call him. Good idea. What's to lose? Everything to gain, nothing to lose, what? It's not a matter of pride. I ran it out of me. I'm running all the bad things out of me, and all that's going to be left is a pure distillation of the good things, which are . . . uh . . . well, for one, lust.

Augusta, blushing at herself, dialed Daniel's number, which she knew by heart.

"Hello?" said his voice. "Hello?"

"Oh . . . uh . . . is this Daniel?"

"Augusta. Well, hello, lady!"

"You recognized my voice!"

"Shouldn't I have? I'm sorry. Who is this?"

Augusta laughed. "You didn't call. Why didn't you call? This is a terrible thing for me to be calling you."

"I think it's wonderful. When shall we get together?"

"But do you want to see me? Were you going to call?"

"Of course I was."

"We'll just talk. Maybe we should just meet and . . . just talk together. It's been so long, and maybe you weren't going to call."

"Okay. You come here tomorrow at one o'clock and we'll just talk. All right? Is that good for you?"

"Yes. All right."

"Till then."

"Bye, Dan."

Augusta hung up the phone, still blushing. I am so bad, she thought. Augusta felt very humiliated with herself.

Bad.

Then she thought about tomorrow at one and was so

happy she was going to see him and have a wonderful lovemaking experience again that she hugged herself for joy. Her pudenda wept to think of it.

After we talk, that is.

Probably we won't talk.

No matter. I'm so happy, so glad. I'm glad I'm bad.

. . . 3

Once again Ephraim and Evalyn sat across from each other. Once again she thought he looked stunning. This time he was dressed in pale blue: pants of a fine, almost velvet-looking corduroy, and a turtleneck jersey of the same blue tone, lighting up the blue of his eyes. He wore a black belt with an ornate silver buckle. His feet were clad in bright blue running shoes.

Evalyn wore a wraparound dress of fine Italian wool in a subdued print.

Nancy had fled this malignant interview. She'd gone to Fantasia Bakery to eat a chocolate cake.

Evalyn had already given Daniel's address and description to Ephraim. "I believe he's involved with some woman other than myself. When you have ascertained who she is, kill her. Make it look like an accident. Run her down in a car."

"That is not my style. Car accidents are messy and uncertain."

"I'm sorry if it offends your delicate sensibilities. We can only hope that you will raise the art of hit-and-run to a higher place in the hierarchy of murder methods, because that is the way I wish it to be done. Secure an untraceable car and abandon it after the accident. The fact that this is not your style makes it less likely that you would ever be connected with it and I with you. Therefore it leaves me totally unconnected."

"Would you hire a bricklayer to set a diamond? No, you would go to a jeweler, the best available jeweler."

"And then I would tell him exactly what I wanted done. I'll pay generously. Money is no object."

"What *is* the object? I'm interested. I like to understand the job I'm doing."

"What a question! Am I to defend myself to you? Justify my desire for her death—make it less sordid, perhaps? How ridiculous."

"Just tell me why you want her dead."

"I want her out of the way. I want him for myself. Totally. It's simple."

"Mightn't there be another girl afterwards? And another?"

"I shall marry him. I see now that I should have married him at once when I had finally found *exactly* what I have always wanted. I should have seized it." She made a seizing motion, tightening her fists. Then she relaxed and smiled. "Good, Mr. Johnstone. I am so glad you made me realize this with your impertinent question."

"You still want her dead?"

"Very much. Yes, that is exactly how I want her. Without fail."

"I never fail, and this is not a job that requires much talent or preparation—which is why I'll only charge you thirty thousand dollars. Fifteen thousand now, the rest after. But I will decide the method according to the character of the mark. Are we agreed?"

"Agreed. Dead then. Dead and disfigured will be fine."

# 4

## . . . . . *Lovers*

AUGUSTA decided to park in the Marina and run across the city to Daniel's. That way she could get in her daily run, and the different terrain would be interesting. After all, her book was to be set in cities; she should accustom herself to city running. In a light pack that she secured around her waist, she put an outfit she could change into afterwards. After talking? Oh, never mind about the talking.

Talking went by the board entirely. As soon as she stepped into Daniel's apartment, he enfolded her in his arms—and there she remained, one way or another, for the duration.

And so it went for visit after visit. Augusta ran to and from the embraces of her lover, got to know San Francisco very well, got very good at running hills, at making love. She really shouldn't have run back to her car each time, because she found that after such prolonged lovemaking, she fell into a sort of trance that left her with an attention span of zero, totally unaware of her surroundings or of the activity of people and cars. More than once she came close to death by automobile.

"Jesus, lady, watch where you're going!"

"Look out!"

"Honk!"

"Pardon me, miss, but did you know that you narrowly escaped being hit by that car?"

"No. No, I didn't realize at all. Golly, how terrifying. Where was I?"

Zonked. She was sensually and physically zonked. Blissed out.

Augusta, having had so little sexual experience, did not realize that she had accidentally hit upon a phenomenal lover, a man who was really dedicated to the erotic arts and had unusual staying power, recovery power, continuing power.

Evalyn, of course, realized this very well. That's why she was quite willing to do murder to keep him.

Daniel stood alone. He was not a stud; studs are commonplace. A stud was to Daniel what, in the hierarchy of the circus, a freak is to an aerialist. As a lover he had

form, style, poetry, quality, and talent. He had gener-
ousness. He was, as Evalyn said to Nancy, talented in
tenderness.

As well, Daniel released the phenomenal lover who
had lain slumbering in Augusta.

Colette's mother wrote these words in a letter to her
daughter: "I am seized with an admiration that somehow
disturbs me. They say that great lovers feel like that before the object of their passion. Can it be then that, in
my way, I am a great lover? That's a discovery that would
have much astonished my two husbands!"

Maybe, thought Augusta when she read this, everyone
has in them a great lover. They have only to find that
right person or object to release it. But most people
never do. Never! How terribly sad. Probably they don't
think to search for the person or thing that can waken
the sleeping lover within; perhaps they fear to arouse it,
for it can be a wild beast they let loose, a wild, hungry
beast.

No, there was no serious talking with Daniel on the
first visit or any ensuing visits. Dan was not a serious
talker. He was a rather shy man. They talked about su-
perficial things. He might ask her, "Have you got
another earthquake for me?"

"Yes, a terrible one in New Guinea. Nine thousand
dead, six villages destroyed. Another killer quake. It's
not that there are so many quakes this year; it's that
they're all such killers."

"My."

"You're not really interested."

"I'm absolutely fascinated." Then he would take her in his arms and caress her until she sang her garden song of pleasure.

His only flaw as a lover was that he would not speak any words of love to her. This was a terrible disappointment to Augusta, who cherished words so much—her first lover would not say how much he loved her.

"It's against the rules of the bachelors' club," he said.

"Is it because I'm married? Do you want me to leave Duke? I . . . I don't think I could leave my girls for very long."

"And I couldn't take you to sea with me. That's my career. I can't change it midway. I don't want to marry, and I don't believe in love. Love is something you can feel when you're a boy in grammar school. Probably your first puppy love is the closest you ever come to love in your life, when your heart pounds and you can hardly speak for adoration of that little curly-haired girl."

"Really? You really believe that?"

"I really do."

"Didn't you ever almost marry?"

"Yes, I came close once."

"What happened?"

"She was a moaner. We would meet for a drink, and I would always have to listen to what a terrible day she'd had. If by chance I had had a bad day, hers was worse. She should have let me have an awfuller day sometimes."

Augusta laughed.

"If I marry at all, it will be to a rich woman who will look after me in my old age so I don't end up in a nursing home like my poor old mother."

"You would marry for money?" Augusta was shocked and disbelieving.

"That's the only sensible reason to marry. Not yet, though. For sure I'd have to dance attendance on the woman and quit my job. I wouldn't like that now, but I'll go along with it when I'm older."

"I just don't believe you. Still, Duke cares a lot about money too. They say that women are the gold diggers, but I think men like money more."

"They appreciate it more because they have to work so bloody hard to get it. Day in and day out. It's a tread-mill, especially if you have a family and it all gets spent as fast as you make it. At least I can sock some away, although I blew a lot in my misspent youth."

"You're right. Poor Duke. But now it seems like money's all he thinks about."

Disturbed, she fell silent, and then into a light doze. When she awakened she saw that Daniel had also slept. He looked very sweet. She kissed his neck. She kissed his shoulder, under his arm, down his side to that tender meeting place of leg and torso. She kissed his penis and saw it give a little leap. She smiled with delight and took it into her smile, into her delight, excitedly felt it swell. "Look at that, Dan," she said, lifting her face from him and pointing exuberantly to his penis, glistening with her saliva.

"It is such a wonder to me the way it—you—grow so large so soon, some miracle of nature it is. But it makes me feel proud too, as if it's my creation, my sculpture, a work of art, a masterpiece—or mistresspiece, rather. I feel like Leonardo!"

"Hmmm, not bad"—he observed himself judiciously—

"but it needs a little more work, I think." He entered her body and they moved rhythmically together. "Shall we see how it looks now?"

"No. Don't leave me. I beg you not to leave me. Oh!"

When he finally did leave her, after a long and tantric time of love, the mistresspiece was much diminished. "It wouldn't command anything at Sotheby's now," Augusta smiled. "Oh, Daniel, you do make me so happy. You give me so much. Even if you don't love me, I *feel* as though you do. And that's nice. Daniel, maybe even if you can't say you love me, you could express some sort of commitment to me. Something?"

"Very well, what? Got any ideas?"

What indeed? Since he clearly said he wouldn't love her or marry her, what was left? Well, there was doing her jogging book with her, but she didn't want to ask him that yet.

Augusta thought long and hard, and then she smiled. She smiled because it was going to sound silly—and it was silly—yet she felt seriously about it. It seemed an important sort of commitment, something she'd be glad to know about a person, about a friend or lover, a promise she'd be glad to have. So her voice was tremulous as she smiled and said, "I've thought of something. If I die, I want you to come to my funeral, because that's being a good lover. That's what a lover should do—come to my funeral and mourn me, be really sad. Promise you'll do that? Promise?"

"All right. I will. But I'll be the only man there in a veil, and it'll look pretty funny."

She laughed. "You mean you'll still be nervous about me even when I'm dead?"

"I expect to be nervous about you even when *I'm* dead."

Augusta knew he wasn't kidding. He always asked her what she had told her husband about her outings, what excuse she gave, whether Duke ever noticed anything strange or asked anything unusual. He would never call her at her house or write to her. He insisted that she call him from a public booth so his number would not be on her bill. She liked that part. There was something so enchanting about slipping out at night to a phone booth lit with its sweet, mysterious light, a tiny space in which to reach out for the voice of her lover, his dear, delightful phrases issuing through the box, her bosom sighing with pleasure at this intimate night-touching of voices across the bay. (Did the cable go underwater?) She would breathlessly murmur the inconsequential details of her day—so very much to tell, to share—and how interested he was, how charmed he seemed, a response long gone from Duke.

She suspected that Daniel found her odd, disturbing even, but mightn't he be enriched thereby? He seemed to be. And she was so grateful for his interest, his love (though he didn't call it that), grateful most certainly for his embraces, but above all for his being there at the end of the line when she called and for being so pleased to converse with her. This nourished her most of all.

So much so that when she saw an aquatint etching by James Torlakson called *19th Avenue Phone Booth 1:00 A.M.* at the Palace of the Legion of Honor museum, she bought it. It began the long haul back from Hiroshige to the moderns, rekindling her interest in the artistic "now."

But to return to Daniel's many injunctions. He would not step outside his door with her, wouldn't run with her or take her out for a meal. *He wouldn't run with her;* that's what made her saddest, for she had so enjoyed the day they had run together, talking all the while, and she wanted very much to experience it again. Especially since, more and more, she dreamed of doing the IJB with him, even though there was less evidence to support this dream than there had been in the case of Duke (Duke at least would go outdoors with her). But he did think the book was a great idea—he had not said he would *not* do it—and he let her talk about it, listened, seemed interested.

There were many things she wanted to experience with Daniel. But he would not venture abroad with her at all. He even went so far as not to let her stand near the window for fear the house might be watched.

And, of course, it was being watched.

# 5

. . . . . *At Tennessee*
*Valley Cove*

EPHRAIM was diligently watching the apartment house
when Daniel was home and tailing him when he was out.
But he did not discover that Daniel was involved with
any woman other than Evalyn. When he reported as
much to her, she was not convinced. "I trust my intui-
tions. They are never wrong. There is someone."

Ephraim thought it over. He took a walk in Tennessee
Valley Cove, a place he often went to be even more by
himself and to think. It was a lonely, empty place, conducive to contemplation. The narrow valley was hugged

by high, steep hills where fat, shiny black Anguses cropped the grass and ruminated and gave scale to the height and breadth of the hills. When Ephraim had first come here, in the winter, the valley had been green and had reminded him of Wales—like suddenly stepping off the freeway into another nation, silent and pastoral, or even like stepping into another time frame. And yet, if he climbed to the top of that hill to his left, he would behold a metropolis—the whole Bay Area containing millions of people—which made the valley even more magical to Ephraim.

Today, as he followed the slender trail for two miles to the cove, he saw that the cows were huddling under the shade of the oak trees along the dry creek bed. The drought had so dried the wild grasses that the hills had merely a film of growth on them, a delicate web of fibers revealing the rock-hard earth beneath. Where the wildflowers had been tall and rampant, only an odd one appeared—a California poppy looking like a bonsai flower, tiny and stunted, denying its leaves and stem so as to put all its power into the bloom. It was only a fleck of orange on the ground, like something dropped from a pocket.

But Ephraim liked all this. This dry sparseness, this hunger, appealed to his nature. Anything too flamboyantly beautiful actually caused him pain.

He walked along and puzzled over "Daniel's other woman." No woman ever came to Daniel's apartment, and Daniel only left the building to see Evalyn or to meet with men who were obviously old cronies, seagoing persons like himself. As for the other two apartments in the building, he had established that an elderly woman lived in one, a homosexual in the other. Neither tenant received young women.

Yet he had to respect Evalyn's insistence; she was no fool. It was very curious.

He heard footsteps behind him. Even in his brown study he was alert to everything. But he didn't bother to turn. They were light running steps. It would be some boy runner. The only other people who came to this cove were runners, or bird watchers hung round with cameras and binoculars.

The runner flashed by him, a girl. She wore shorts, shirt, and hat. He noted her fine body, beautiful legs, natural gait—graceful, an ecto-meso like himself, one of the chosen.

Ruminating: There was, in fact, a jogger who came to the Vallejo Street apartment. In a bright green sweat suit. He'd been amazed to see her actually run up that incredibly steep hill, amazed and admiring. She . . . !

Ephraim stopped and stood still as the light dawned. She—the jogger was a she, was a woman. There was something so androgynous about a jogger in a sweat suit that, in the cataloguing of visitors to the building, his mind always listed "jogger." He'd never granted it a sex, never considered the jogger to be "the woman" because . . . well, because one doesn't go to a romantic assignation in a green sweat suit, flushed of face, and wet with perspiration. It was unheard of.

He was making apologies for himself. The fact was, it was inexcusable that he had let this possibility get by him. It was appalling that he, like some tyro, some novice, had been snookered by the very trick he played himself! The woman was so outrageously noticeable that he hadn't noticed her.

Ephraim took up a sharp stone from the path and scraped it viciously along the length of his forearm. The blood bubbled up, streamed down his arm and hand, shockingly red in the colorless setting. There, that would raise a scab to be a palpable reminder until this job was done. Very likely it would leave a scar too, so he'd always remember the time he'd been a fool. He'd thought this job was so easy, so stupid and unchallenging, that he'd only put half a mind to it.

The interstice of two hills contained the blue of the ocean growing larger now as he walked toward it, opening suddenly to the lagoon, which was covered with a multitude of seabirds and ducks. Beyond the lagoon was the wild, cliff-encumbered cove. The roar of ocean jarring upon continent assailed his ears.

DANGEROUS WATER. NO LIFEGUARD ON DUTY.

On the small beach were a horsewoman, a black fisherman, two nude sunbathers, and the girl runner, who, having thrown off her hat and shoes, was standing in the surf. Her long hair lashed about her in the breeze, long red hair . . .

*He knew that hair.*

She turned and walked toward him, and Ephraim got a jolt. This was the very woman. He felt at once relieved and alarmed—glad that he had identified her, alarmed to be seen by her.

She walked toward him, saw him . . . smiled! She

smiled and paused and stopped before him. "Hello," she said, friendly as could be.

Ephraim experienced a flick almost of fear.

He turned away.

"I'm sorry." She blushed, so that her face, already pink from her running, turned red. "I thought I knew you from somewhere but . . . but, my goodness! You've hurt yourself! Look at your arm!"

"It's nothing," said Ephraim through his teeth.

"It certainly is! Here, please, just sit down a minute and I'll bring some seawater to clean it with, to disinfect it—the iodine and all, you know, the salt. That's a horrible cut." She ran to fill her hat with water. She bent down to the trough of the wave. The next wave curled over her and knocked her under.

It seemed to Ephraim that everything happened too fast; he was in another time frame, a film. It was as if a film were being shown to him: his coming to the cove, the blueness after the taupe of the valley, the dazzling sea, the horse, the black fisherman casting out his thread of line, the girl coming towards him with her wild hair and high color—not a girl, though, a woman, *the* woman, his victim—smiling at him, friendly, then embarrassed, then concerned, going to succor him, her slight frame bowing to the wave, then taken away by it, gone.

Suddenly he entered the film, was himself in the ocean wresting the woman from the entanglement of waves, feeling angry and bewildered, thinking, This is wrong, this is crazy, incredible, not to be believed.

The nude sunbathers ran up with towels for each of them, their genitals bobbing and swaying. Ephraim thrust his towel away and said, "Look after her!" Then, with long strides, he put the cove behind him.

That evening, at dinner, Augusta told Duke and Val and Lee all about her experience at the cove.

"I was bending down to fill my hat with water, and this wave grabbed me. It just sort of grabbed me, and I was completely helpless; I couldn't do a thing. I couldn't right myself. It pulled me under and whirled me all around. I tried not to swallow water, waiting for the moment I'd hit air and could grab a breath, all the time thinking, My God, it's going to sweep me right out to sea like those freak waves we're always reading about along the coast here that pluck people from beaches and cliffs and just run away with them. It was stupid of me, because there are signs all over that cove saying how dangerous it is, and here I was losing my life, all for a man I didn't know, who hadn't wanted me to help him in the first place, who obviously didn't need help, never had or would need help in all his life, deplored and despised help of any kind, so that it was absolutely perverse of me to have been getting him seawater in the first place! Anyhow, he could very well have gone and put his whole arm in the water by himself. He was perfectly mobile, for God's sake, his legs weren't hurt. The whole thing was ridiculous!

"Yes, ridiculous. And yet, and yet . . . I was so *moved* by him. His arm looked awful. He himself looked so sort of ashen-faced and terrible. . . . Look, see this, this horrible scrape on my inner arm? You will say, of course, that I got it when I was being whirled under by the wave, but truly I think it is an example of body empathy, one of the physical *siddhis* that Mike Murphy talks about whereby one's own body can express the physical hurt of another person. Stigmata are an extreme example of that. You may snort, Duke, but it is true that since I have begun to run, I have experienced altered states . . . well, never mind, I know you hate my running talk. But I do think this is body empathy because how could I have scraped the *inner* arm, and I was so very moved by him. I felt related.

"Anyhow, I went to get the water. I guess my maternal instincts were aroused, or maybe just my foolishness was fired, because whenever I see someone so really terribly stern it brings out the silliness in me; I want to make them laugh. So there I was in the waves getting murdered, when I felt these incredibly strong arms grab me, just pluck me away with the exact same strength the wave had shown. He stood in the roiling surf, not being displaced or toppled, and just plucked me up into the life-giving air. He carried me ashore and placed me—or rather flung me, it seemed—onto the sand. My shirt had literally been torn off by the water and stony sand, so that I felt perfectly comfortable with the two nude men who came and attended to me. 'Take care of her,' my savior ordered them, and marched off. I never even thanked him. 'Who was that masked man?' I asked the nudes, who were swaddling me in towels."

Augusta looked about at the solemn family faces. "Wasn't that an exciting story? Life is so exciting these days. I feel like an entirely new person. It's really exhilarating to almost die. And to think, Duke, it wasn't so many months ago that I was afraid to leave the house alone, and now I go running all around, narrowly escaping death at every turn. Did I tell you about all the times I almost got hit by cars in the city recently?"

Duke seemed to come alive at this. "You've been running around the city? Why?"

"Why . . . er . . . for my book."

"Book? What book?"

"What book? How can you say, 'What book?' when you know very well I'm planning an International Jogging Book, a running guide to the capital cities of the world, a physical, marital, and mystical odyssey . . . "

"I thought you'd given up that idea."

"Because you think what you want to think, that's why. And you don't even express any concern or interest in my almost losing my life, but only say, 'What book?' What book, for God's sweet sake! What book? What book? Oh, good grief! What book!"

"Your mother is not herself," Duke said to the girls.

"I am myself. I am myself. I am completely myself." Augusta burst into tears and left the table. She went to the bed in her half-room.

The girls came and kissed her and said they loved her and were very glad she hadn't been killed and thought it was wonderful that she was running all around and planning a book about it.

"And I believe in the body empty, too," said Lee.

"Oh, thank you, my darlings. I'm so glad that you believe in my running and my book. How I wish your father did. I so much want to do this book. Will you be all right without me if I go off running around the world?

Naturally someone would look after you, but I do worry about leaving you both. I never have."

"We could stay with friends. It would be fun."

"Really?"

"Sure," said Val. "Anyhow, it looks like I'll be off to college in the fall."

"And if Daddy doesn't go," said Lee, "then I'll take care of him."

Duke remained at the dinner table, considering. He wondered if the incident at Tennessee Valley Cove had really happened: the extremely tall, red-haired young man with the bloody arm, Augusta getting him water in her hat (her hat!), the freak wave, the rescue, the two other men (naked!) giving her towels while the rescuer walked away. It all sounded very unlikely. Then she adds that she's narrowly escaped other deaths recently. Mightn't this be another symptom of the same deep disturbance that produced the agoraphobia? Now, instead of being timid, almost a recluse, Augusta imagines herself an adventurer risking death at every turn, a swashbuckler, and actually seems to be seriously considering doing this strange book—this really idiotic book—as if to give some meaning to her behavior.

Duke sighed. He supposed he should do something, but what? She wasn't doing any harm, certainly. She was still keeping up her duties in the house. Barely. More and more the girls seemed to be going to Jack-in-the-Box for dinner. He looked carefully around the part of the house he could see from where he sat. Yes, it did seem to him that slightly, almost imperceptibly, things were beginning to go to hell. As soon as she stopped crying, he would tell her to shape up. Women should not be pampered in their delusions; they should be warned. If she'd told him about the agoraphobia, he'd have driven it away by belittling it. He'd have forbidden it. Though it wasn't such a bad thing, really—a lot better than this new reckless behavior.

When all was quiet in the half-room, Duke went in, but Augusta was asleep and he decided not to disturb her. He would talk to her tomorrow. He sighed again. It was really too bad that a man who had a lot of business worries couldn't depend on his wife to act normally and keep things running smoothly at home.

He paced around restlessly, every so often running his finger along a table or shelf to measure the dust. Had she really been running around the city? The actual streets? Did she run through Union Square? The financial district? What if one day he was going to a business lunch with friends and she came running by?

What if the wave, supposing there was a wave, had taken her out to sea? He and the girls would be here now, wondering where she was, and she would be under the sea, dead, being jawed by a shark possibly. Duke shivered. How horrible. But these things did happen. She was right about the freak waves. They were indebted to the red-haired man, if he existed, for life.

# 6

..... *Lovers, Continued*

"SO THE next morning," Augusta told Daniel a few days later, "Duke gave me this . . . this . . . talking-to. He said that he thought I'd got much too carried away with all my running—that I was letting everything to to hell around the house and that he really thought I'd imagined the incident at Tennessee Valley Cove. Now, I ask you, how can you imagine almost drowning? Granted I could have exaggerated it in my mind or in my narration, but the very fact someone had to pull me out proves I was in a bad way, doesn't it? He seems to doubt that someone did pull me out. You believe me, don't you?"

"Sure." Daniel sighed and poured himself a Glen Garry.

"Well, that's good. I apologized to him for screaming about the jogging book, because the truth is I hadn't been telling him much about it since he'd been so unresponsive to the idea, but I am completely serious about it. I am going to do it. You believe me, don't you?"

"I believe you."

"That's good."

Actually, like Duke, Daniel was having some misgivings. He wished that the affair would run more smoothly just as Duke wished the house would. He wished that he didn't have to keep feeling so nervous about Augusta, that she would be more ordinary. These tales she told were amusing—but also disturbing. He had a sense that something awful was going to happen to Augusta and he would be involved. It was too bad this was such a long leave. He felt about ready to go back to sea right now, caught as he was between the two women: Evalyn, who was getting heavy, and Augusta, who was getting improbable. Maybe he should take a little voyage for fun, go down to Mexico or up to Alaska—sailor's holiday.

He freshened his drink. "Maybe we should cool it a little, you and I," Daniel said gently. "It sounds as though Duke is getting savvy."

"No. No, I'm sure he's not."

"It would go badly with me if he found out about us. He has a lot of power and influence in the industry."

"He does?" Augusta was surprised by this view of Duke but felt too hurt by his wanting to "cool it" to explore the surprise. Of course, she reasoned, Daniel's job was important, but wasn't she important, too?

"Another thing," Daniel said. "I have a friend, a woman friend, Evalyn, who is very attached to me. I wouldn't want her to learn about us either."

"Daniel!" Augusta felt as if she'd been sandbagged.

"She is someone I knew before you," he said nicely.

"But, Daniel . . . !"

"It is exactly like you and Duke. I am not the only man in your life, am I?"

"No, but . . . but . . . oh, God!" Augusta began to weep. Daniel patted her clumsily, feeling upset by her tears. "It seems all I do these days is cry," Augusta said, trying to stop. He caressed her, but she moved away from him. "No, no, just . . . just tell me about her. I want to know all about her."

Daniel lay down on the bed and set his drink on his chest. Augusta remained standing.

"Well," he said. "She's smart, attractive, about ten years older than you, and she drinks Mumms Extra Dry."

"Is she going to support you in your old age?"

"It looks like it."

"She's rich?"

"Immensely."

"Congratulations," said Augusta. Suddenly she felt old and bitter and depraved. She had a vision of herself back in early March, happy with her home, her art books, her daughters, puttering in her garden, never going anywhere except to town—a nice person, a good wife and mother, growing old gracefully. Now here she was, deep in iniquity, caught in a web of deception and lies, driven by lust, risking her marriage and her life. And all for what? Well, for the jogging book, she guessed. It began with the jogging book. Maybe she was crazy. That was what Duke had been suggesting the other morning—that any woman who would run around cities to write a jogging book that nobody wanted was crazy.

Even if she was crazy—and she wasn't—she was going to speak out and not succumb as she had to the hideous disease that had previously confined her. Confined her! Just so! She *wasn't* happy back in early March, not at all. She had been confined, imprisoned, and she had broken free. Her spirit had flown. It wasn't easy. Her spirit kept bumping into things, but she was free. And alive! She felt awfully much more alive, she felt really good—in fact, her body felt wonderful. She loved her body. And all her senses were so wonderfully heightened. Every day was a new adventure for her.

Last week she had been running on the mountain, an hour run on the Matt Davis Trail, and as she finished up she came upon a fellow harrier who was ending a run down the railroad grade. He was dressed in white shorts and shirt, had a red bandanna around his head Indian fashion, and his face was absolutely gleeful. He began talking at once. "I ran all the way up to the top of the mountain from the town square," he said, "and now I've just run down to here. Two hours and ten minutes it took me. My legs feel a bit watery. It was an awful lot of up, two thousand feet elevation from the square, I guess, but I feel great. I'm so glad I did it. It was my forty-third birthday present to myself. I'm so happy. I feel just wonderful!"

Why would a man give himself such a long, lonely, painful ordeal for a birthday present? Augusta knew why.

It was a totally life-affirming present to oneself at the marking off of another year towards death.

When they exchanged names, Augusta smiled, because she had met him some years before as a distinguished scientist, a friend of her best friend, now totally unrecognizable as the person he'd been. As was she, he said.

All these thoughts whirled through Augusta's mind just after she bitterly said, "Congratulations," to Daniel, so that he was surprised and relieved to see her frown turn to a smile in a matter of moments.

She sat down beside him on the bed and tenderly stroked the hair on his chest and stomach. "Of course I'm not the only person in your life. How could I be? You've lived without me for all these years. I guess I haven't wanted to think about your life before me, or even during me. I'm glad she's rich. And I'm awfully glad she's old. I shouldn't let it bother me and cast a pall on our time together. I should be . . . sophisticated, I guess, and take it all in stride. I should be able to divorce the physical expression of love from love itself, make love to you without loving you—fucking, I guess it's called. *Fuck* is such a hostile-sounding word, I think. You say I have Duke as well as you but . . . I haven't had sex with Duke since you returned. Probably he hasn't even noticed. But I have been that honest with myself, at least. God knows, I'm dishonest enough to Duke, to myself, maybe even to you. Maybe I say I love you simply because the idea of sex without love is repugnant to me, and therefore I have to imagine I love you."

"Could be," Daniel said. "Could be, lady. I don't think

you could have loved me the first time, since we hadn't even seen each other for years. But it was very nice. It's always nice with us."

"It is. It's incredibly nice!"

I'm going to have to leave Duke, Augusta realized. I can't go on like this.

It was a terrifying thought, and when it came she threw herself on Daniel so as to expunge it from her mind.

Daniel had to react quickly to keep his drink from spilling, but he was an old hand at saving drinks. He set it on the bedside table with one hand while he received her with the other.

Addressing himself appreciatively to Augusta's lively, wanton ardor, he tried for a moment to look into his heart and discovered that there certainly was a soft spot there for Augusta, a spot that she had touched and made soft in a way no woman had in his adult life. She was so openhearted and innocent. He would hate to think that he was corrupting any of that, but he rather thought not. The openhearted and open-minded people are the strong ones, he decided. They have the most power because they give instead of take. They give and gain while the takers lose. Her heart would not be hardened. Instead, it was his poor old world-weary heart that was being softened. No, he would not feel responsible for Augusta, would not worry about her. She was way ahead of them all.

# 7

. . . . . *Three More
Conversations*

VAL *was* a little worried about her mother, and when
Augusta got home from the city that day, Val asked,
"Any near deaths today?"

Augusta laughed. "Oh, the usual number. Something
there is about a runner that brings out the axe murderer
in everybody."

She went to the refrigerator and got out the pitcher of
cranberry juice for them both. "I guess it's the natural

antagonism people feel towards the incomprehensible. And there is nothing mitigating about a runner that someone could choose to pity or admire instead of hate. It might be acceptable if I was running a race or running to get somewhere on time, but just running for no reason makes me a public nuisance, a botheration in the brains of the populace, so they honk, throw things, call derisively, set dogs upon me, see how close they can come to me with their cars without actually bloodying the fenders . . . "

"Maybe," Val suggested, "it hurts them to see you run because they know they can't use their bodies for getting places and can only drive."

Augusta stretched out on her back on the rug, her head on her hands. "The weird thing is that I keep seeing that amazing red-haired man who saved me. Today I saw him twice, once in the city and once right here in Mill Valley. That's quite extraordinary, considering I never saw him before. Could I be imagining it? Of course, your father thinks I imagined him in the first place, but I didn't. Actually, when I saw him at the cove, I had the feeling I had seen him before, but I can't think where. I even said hello to him, feeling he was somehow familiar. It's odd. Maybe I knew him in another life."

"Did he see you? Today, I mean."

"No. I called to him. I tried to get his attention, but he didn't see me. Of course, I was running and he was driving. He has the most imperturbable face—like an image, like a mask."

"That's what you said to the nudes: 'Who was that masked man?' "

"Yes, but that was a joke, an allusion to the Lone Ranger, who always used to ride away before anybody could thank him, and at the end of the program—this was radio—the person would say, 'Who was that masked man?' and someone would answer, 'Why, that was the Lone Ranger,' and then in the distance you'd hear, 'Hiyo, Silver, Awa-a-a-y.' "

"Oh."

"Ah, those were the days, Val, when out of the past came the thundering hoofbeats . . . "

"Okay, Mom, that's enough. I'm going to read now, okay?"

"Okay." Augusta was thoughtful. "That's probably why I said it, though, because he looks so masked. He's awfully young to look so masked. Awfully young and beautiful."

"Just don't get obsessed. Daddy says you're obsessed with running."

"He does, does he? Well, what I call 'caring about,' he calls 'obsessed' because he really knows how to make things sound bad instead of good. He's really gifted at that. I could say to him 'Isn't it a lovely day today!' and he'd say I was obsessed with the weather. Which reminds me, did you hear about the man who woke up and thought it looked nice out, so he left it out all day?"

They both giggled.

. . . **2**

Duke walked in, looked down at Augusta on the rug,

and said, "Any near escapes from death today?" Only he didn't say it with cheerful inquisitiveness, as Val had. To Augusta it sounded sarcastic, condescending, demeaning. It roused the dormant axe murderer in her.

"Five," she said, "and one to grow on."

"Well, aren't we snippy tonight." He cracked a beer and stepped over her to go to the living room, where he turned on the new television.

I hate him, Augusta thought. I'm really beginning to *hate* him.

"Do you ever try to hit runners with your Mercedes, Duke? Really, I'd be interested to know. Do you?"

"Only on odd Thursdays," he said. Then he said, "Sh!" as was his custom when engaged by the TV.

Augusta thought of Daniel and how he was always so happy to see her, how he smiled and hugged her when she came to his door. He was so nice, so loving. He would never step over her and turn on the television. Actually, she supposed she should be glad that Duke hadn't stepped *on* her.

Suddenly Duke asked, "Augusta, if you have been running in the city, would you mind telling me how you get to the city?"

She felt a shot of fear. She was so taken aback that she didn't answer quickly or naturally. "Bus," she quavered, wondering wildly if the bus strike had ended.

"Hmmmnnm" was his response to that. "It's funny, because I could have sworn I saw you in a blue sports car today. I guess I was wrong, wasn't I?"

"No, not wrong. Just imagining, like I imagined the red-haired man, according to you," said Augusta, quickly recovering her spirit from its last bump. She sat up. "And I must say my powers of imagination certainly are formidable, because I have seen him again and again since that day at the cove. If I wasn't a sensible, level-headed housewife, I could imagine that he was the Angel of Life, because I almost lost my life the moment of first seeing him and I've seen him so often since then as I go about escaping death from maniac motorists."

"Don't you mean the Angel of Death?" asked Val, looking up from her book. "I never heard of the Angel of Life. Although why would an Angel of Death save you from drowning?"

"So a car could get me, I guess."

"Or maybe so you could get a car," Duke suggested heavily, "a little blue one."

"I do not have a little blue car."

"Sure, Mom," said Val ironically.

"Does she?" Duke asked Val.

"I didn't say anything," Val said, pretending to be deep in her book again.

"Does your mother have a blue sports car?" Duke asked as Lee was entering the living room.

"No, because if she did it would be so mean of her not to give us rides in it. *So mean!*" And Lee glared pointedly at her mother.

Augusta crept away to her half-room and got the Hiroshige out from under the mattress. She contemplated it for a long while, hoping to find surcease from her troubles.

She didn't.

What am I doing? she asked herself. What am I doing

to my life and my marriage? What is all this running for? Could it be an illness, not a healing? Destructive, not creative? Even if it isn't, Duke thinks it is, so the result will be the same; the shadow of incarceration will hang over me once again, as it always did for Mummy. The truth is, I've never behaved normally, but whereas previously I pretended to be normal, hid my eccentricities, now I flaunt them. But I don't think that I'm odd. I'm coming to believe that everyone else is. I'm the normal one because I exult in my body, feel full of life, love, joy. I'm made to feel antisocial by people who are the true abnormals, surly monsters who evolved from a society dedicated to nervousness. But I see that Duke will never come around to my way of thinking and being unless something extraordinary happens to jolt him out of his entrenchment. An earthquake! Ah! Yes. That must be why I keep counting quakes, hoping that a natural disaster will come and effect a change that I can't quite manage on my own.

. . . 3

Several days later, Ephraim met again with Evalyn. Nancy was there in the diplomat suite when he arrived, and she showed him in.

"Good morning, Mr. Johnstone. This is Nancy O'Hara. Nancy, please sit down. I wish you to remain. You may speak freely in front of Nancy. I have no secrets from her."

"Thanks, Evalyn," said Nancy, "but I guess I'll give this

meeting the go-by. I don't care to be an accessory, thanks."

"You already are an accessory, Nancy, you bitch. Sit down. If you've committed a crime in your heart, you've as good as done the deed. So has this deed been done, and you were present when I committed it. And don't say, 'What heart?' I'm not in the mood for your jokes. This is business." Evalyn gestured towards Ephraim. "Nancy, we have here a very distinguished professional, without peer in his field. He has never failed."

"He's young yet," said Nancy, sitting down resignedly in a corner chair.

"I consider excellence more admirable in the young. Excellence then becomes a thing prodigious, a God-given ability, whereas most professionals become 'the best' through age, experience, and application."

"She meant that by being young I have had less opportunity to fail," said Ephraim.

"I know what she meant," Evalyn snapped. She was in a horrible humor. "Though perhaps you have found your opportunity now. You did not feel, as I recall, that this job would be any sort of challenge. I think you said something to the effect that it would not require much talent. Why, then, Mr. Johnstone, have two long weeks gone by without my hearing that the thing is done?"

"I expect to take my time," Ephraim replied cooly. "First I had to make the identification. I couldn't get a fix on the subject for a long while. Away from the apartment, Daniel saw only you or men friends and, although he did spend long hours at home, no one appeared to visit. Then I realized it was the runner."

"The runner?" Evalyn turned wondering eyes to Nancy. "Good God, it's a man."

"This is San Francisco, after all," said Nancy.

"No, it's a woman," said Ephraim. "She runs to and from his place in a green sweat suit."

"How extraordinary."

"Forest green," he added for no reason. "She is about five feet six, slim, has long red hair, and looks to be about thirty years old—though she may be older or, for that matter, younger. It's hard to tell with her. So, if there is a woman, it has to be this runner. But I have no proof. I have never seen them together. I have never seen her in his room when I observed it through high-powered binoculars. Now, with your permission, I will put a tap on his phone and a recording device under his bed. We will wait until they connect and he uses her name."

"You have my permission. Do you know her name?" As Evalyn spoke, a spasm of hatred contracted her features.

"Yes. It was difficult to tail a running woman. I couldn't follow her on foot, walking," he continued wryly, "and it would be an obvious tail if I followed her running. I managed to stay with her, or rather ahead of her, in my car until she picked up her car. Then I followed her to Mill Valley—"

Evalyn cut him off abruptly. "That's enough. I don't want to know her name or anything more about her. As long as you have the information, that's fine." She stood up and smiled falsely, a rictus. "Well, I was right, wasn't I? I'm not happy about it, but my unhappiness is assuaged somewhat by being right. I *love* to be right. It's the next best thing to orgasm. And champagne," she added, signaling Nancy to fill her glass, taking pleasure in watching Nancy try to get out of her chair. "Champagne, Mr. Johnstone?"

"No, thank you." He stood to go.

"Daniel will be lunching with me in an hour. You might go by and place your devices then."

"I will."

"Good luck, Mr. Johnstone," she said, guessing he would abhor the suggestion that luck was involved. After the door had closed on him, she said to Nancy, "I don't think he'll entertain the idea of Lady Luck, do you? For one thing, he doesn't entertain ladies of any nature—does not entertain, period, or be entertained. Very ascetic is our Mr. Johnstone. In another life he would have been a monk." She sipped her champagne and looked out at the view. "Well, Nancy, any comments?"

"There is something he's not telling you," Nancy said.

"My feelings exactly. There is quite a lot he's not telling me. But, at the same time, there's a lot I don't wish to be told."

"Strange to think of a woman running," Nancy said. "I feel he's a bit thrown off by her."

"We will trust in his professionalism. He is the best. I have the best of everything, Nancy. The best friend, the best lover, the best murderer."

The telephone rang. Nancy answered it and passed it to Evalyn. "Daniel."

"Hello, darling," Evalyn greeted him.

"I'm afraid I have to go to Honolulu today. My mother

has died. I'll return in three days, Sunday night. I'm fly-ing out in an hour."

Evalyn felt enraged and frustrated, but she was able to say the correct thing. "My sympathies, Daniel. I'm deep-ly distressed for you. Is there anything I can do?"

"No. She was old."

"You must stay in my condominium. I'll call ahead."

"No, thanks."

"But of course you will."

"I'll probably stay with family."

"Where exactly?"

"I'll just see when I get there."

"Well, do let me know. Call me from Honolulu."

"I'll try. See you Monday. Bye."

Evalyn slammed down the phone in a fury. "He's going to Hawaii. If she's going with him I'll . . . "

"Kill her?"

"Shut up! I'm going to see that forest green sweat suit stained blood red. Now. Before that plane leaves. Never mind proof. Quickly, Nancy. We must advise Ephraim. Run after him."

"Are you kidding?"

"Run, I said!"

"Me run? How? *You* run."

"How dare you!"

"Evalyn, I'm not being insubordinate. I'm only being sensible. I cannot run. It is an accomplishment for me to walk. You must go after him yourself."

"I can't."

"Why not?"

"I . . . it wouldn't be appropriate."

"Because you're so rich, Evalyn? Is that it? I'm too fat to run and you're too rich. A multimillionaire does not run—especially after her hired assassin." Nancy began to laugh. She fell on the couch laughing, her stomach blubber sending out whirlpool waves of merriment to her bosoms, thighs, and chins. "Here we sit, my friend. Who of us is the more burdened? Which is worse, being too fat or too rich?"

"Neither is as bad as having a price on your head. Take down this telegram and send it right off."

Evalyn began to dictate.

# 8

### . . . . . *Ephraim Musing*

EPHRAIM, going down in the Fairmont elevator, considered the irony that, for once, he needed "good luck" very much indeed. Never before had a job revolved so relentlessly around chance. This job, in fact, was a total mess. He was making a complete botch of it.

Augusta had been impossible. She had ways of absolutely disappearing. When she wasn't disappearing, she was running right towards him because she had seen him, recognized him, and wanted to speak with him. Then he would have to appear not to see her. He would virtually have to hide from her, and by so doing, he would lose her. It was exasperating. If he had cut himself for every time he'd been a fool since that day at the cove, he would have been a mass of wounds. That cut was the beginning of the whole problem. But the way she could spot him was amazing. And the way she could vanish! It was like O Sensei. Maybe she was an *aikidoka* as well as a runner.

Thinking of that once more reminded him of the scene in the *dojo* with his father. Was Augusta his lost mother? No, he had already killed his mother by being born—a born killer. But if he must kill her again, he would. He had tried to hurt his father and failed. Instead, his father had embraced him. Just as Augusta was trying to do. She wanted to embrace him, and thank him for saving her life. It was all such a joke, such a poor joke. But his mind was taking an unhealthy turn, dwelling on her this way. Next thing he knew he'd get eczema again.

It was then that Ephraim remembered seeing Augusta at the Ormsby House. He had seen her and noticed her, and she had looked at him, at his diseased cheeks. Yes, for sure that had been this very woman. It was uncanny. Uncanny! And that's why she had approached him on the beach. "I'm sorry, I thought I knew you from somewhere," she'd said.

And the next thing he knew he was saving her life although he'd just determined she was his victim. Of course, he hadn't the proof then, still hadn't, but he knew she was the one.

That incident on the beach pointed up all his feelings about death as the Great Snatcher. In his work he only continued to carry out death's intention of ruthlessly, haphazardly snatching a life away for no reason. In the actual act of killing he brought all of his professional and personal self to the fore; all his intelligence and training culminated in that moment of murder, and yet, strangely, at that moment he never felt less himself. He was only an instrument of death—not Ephraim. It was almost as if he donned one of those primitive masks that so interested him and became a disembodied demon as he eradicated life with total indifference, feeling nothing. Nothing.

So it goes, he thought. One minute a person's alive, the next minute he's dead by a fluke, a freak of nature or society, by an assassin's bullet or by wind, wave, war, fire, automobile, disease, crime, or earthquake. Look at all the thousands being killed this year by the actual movement of the earth beneath their feet. It makes my contribution almost nil.

Why had he saved Augusta? Was it some instinct to preserve? Some reflex action? Or had he *wanted* to save her? If so, why? Could there have been a reason?

Well, she had gone into the water for his sake. To succor him. Which was sort of a reflex in itself. Someone like Augusta was nice enough to have that reflex, to act upon it, and she was odd enough to do something bizarre with it, like turn right around and walk into the sea to fill her hat.

Ephraim felt the twitch of an unfamiliar facial muscle, an infinitesimal smile.

Her action was so kind and so childlike that his reflex once the wave hit her was to go to her rescue.

They say there are angels watching over drunks and children. Ergo, he was Augusta's angel. Or had been momentarily, giving her an allowance of extra time. Now her time was to be up.

He stepped out of the elevator and strode through the majestic lobby, out the doors to his car, which was parked by Grace Cathedral.

It will not be easy, he cautioned himself. Augusta will know me now. I will not be a disembodied demon to her. She will see me coming and recognize me and not understand. That sweet face of hers will be horrified and disbelieving. Worse, she may look at me as she did on the beach—with concern and pity because I have hurt myself, as a mother might have looked at me if I'd ever had a mother. She wants to dress my wounds, cherish me. And all this is dangerous simply because I might once again react adversely, in a reflex of . . . of . . . whatever the hell it was a reflex of.

The answer, then, is to hit her at a safe distance.

Safe! What do I mean, safe? What am I afraid of?

Ephraim drove to Daniel's, placed the bugs in his apartment, and returned home to Strawberry Point, where he found a telegram from Evalyn.

"They've gone to Honolulu for three days. Follow. Stay Hale Kalani. Will contact you."

# 9

. . . . . *At Duke's Attic*

ANOTHER intuitive bull's-eye for Evalyn. Augusta *was* going to Honolulu with Daniel. She was with him when he got the call about his mother, and after determining it was a happy release for the old girl, she clapped her hands with glee and said, "I'll come with you, Daniel. It will be a chance for an International Jogging Route. Honolulu, Oahu, Hawaii. Oh, boy!"

"And what do you tell Duke?"

"I tell him the truth, that I am researching my book."

"We have to leave this afternoon, lady. That's pretty

sudden. I gather you've never traveled more than thirty miles from home by yourself. Now, on the very day of departure, you're announcing a four-thousand-mile weekend journey. Don't you think that's a little out of character? Won't Duke wonder?"

"True. Good point. But it will prepare Duke for the greater surprise of my departure on a hundred-thousand-mile journey for the rest of my life. One way!"

Augusta twirled around the room. "I'll nip home and get some of my traveler's checks. I shall pay my own way, of course."

"You have traveler's checks just sitting at home in the event of my mother dying?"

"Yes, thousands of dollars' worth. It's the advance to myself on my jogging book."

"Thousands? Are you at all familiar with the savings bank system whereby money, if placed in an account, accrues interest in a way that traveler's checks never will?"

"Yes, but—well, it's complicated to explain." Augusta's forehead creased with distress.

"Then don't," he said kindly.

"So I'll just go home, get my money, some clean running clothes, a pretty nightie. I'll arrange everything with the girls, and then I'll come back to the city and go by Duke's office to tell him I'm off. Do you know that I've never seen Duke's office?"

"Nothing surprises me."

"I've never seen it. But it's not entirely his fault. I was always too afraid to come to town. Not that he ever asked me to."

"He must take you out to dinner sometimes."

"Never. He says he has to eat out so much on his travels that he loves to have home cooking when he's home."

"Clever," said Daniel.

"Yes," said Augusta sadly. "And I believed him. He was always so convincing. Well, because it was true. He does love my cooking. But that way he gets the best of both worlds, and I just get my own world."

Augusta was pensive.

"I can remember a time when we did go out to dinner because some friends came to town. Duke grabbed the check. I was so surprised. Then, at the first of the month, he deducted it from my allowance."

"That's pretty impressive," Daniel said. "He should write a husband's manual. It would sell like hot cakes."

"Well, I've purposely not talked much to you about Duke so as not to add to my disloyalty, and I shouldn't start now." She went decisively to the door. "Shall I meet you at the plane?"

"Good idea. I'll get the tickets."

"I'll pay you back, though." Augusta laughed. "This is so exciting. Think of it—Hawaii!" She threw her arms around his neck and gave him a big kiss. "Oh, Daniel, thank you! Thank you for letting me come. I would be afraid to make this first big break all by myself. This will give me courage. See you at four!"

Augusta went home, packed a bag, kissed the girls— who were thrilled about her trip and jealous too, of course—kissed them many times, with many repeated injunctions to: "Be good, look after your father, please eat, don't leave burners on, lock the doors at night, don't open the door to strangers, if anyone calls and just breathes, don't breathe back," etc., etc.

With a sinking heart she went out the door saying the old childish litany, "Good-bye house, 'bye paintings, books, rugs, bushes. Good-bye cherry tree." She hugged the cherry tree (truly) and thought, if I die in Hawaii, if the plane crashes, I'll never see this dear place again, this dear place and my darling children. She kissed them both again.

She was in the car, and Val and Lee were standing by it with funny expressions before she realized. "Oh, uh, I bought this car."

"So we see," said Val.

"I'm sorry. It was a lousy thing to do without telling you."

"It sure was," said Lee.

"Pretty shitty," said Val.

"You're right. I'll explain when I get back. I have a lot to explain when I get back, but first I have to go so I'll know I *can* go. I'm sort of scared, really, going off like this." She looked to her children for comfort. She was leaving the nest. It was terrifying.

"You'll be fine," said Val. "You'll have a wonderful time."

"Thank you. I love you both. And I'll give you lots of rides when I get back, Lee. And Val can learn to drive it herself. Now don't forget . . . "

"Just go!" said Val, encouraging her with a pushing gesture.

She went.

She went to the city, parked at the Stockton Street garage, and made her way briskly to Duke's office, which was in a building across from Gump's. She imagined a cold, dank, cramped, airless attic. Something out of Dickens—not so squalid as to be Quilpian but mean enough to be Scroogian.

She went in the narrow entranceway and saw that he indeed was on the top floor, the attic.

The elevator shuddered upwards, and as always in elevators, she wondered how long it would be before someone found her if she got stuck between floors.

When the door opened, she expected to find herself in a scroungy hallway with various doors to select from. Instead, she stepped out into a magnificent reception area.

"I couldn't believe it," she said later to Daniel during the flight. "It was sort of a cross between the Garden Court of the Sheraton Palace and the Taj Mahal. Really! I kept looking for the reflecting pools. It was so excessively lavish. I expected a string quartet to appear from behind the oriental screen and start tuning up their instruments while a servant rolled in the receptionist's coffee break of flaming cherries jubilee. You should have seen the plants. Orchids even! Huge palms. Not plants, trees! He has a service that takes care of them. And when I think of my poor plants on the porch that I was always so proud to show to Duke, my wispy ferns and violets whose every bloom would send me into ecstasies of artistic achievement."

"Leonardo again," said Daniel, smiling.

"I wish I could kiss you right now," said Augusta, detoured from her account of Duke's attic, feeling suddenly aroused.

"We could join the mile-high club, whose membership has done it on a jet."

"Really? I never heard of such a thing. What a world we live in! I wonder how large the membership is. I think I'd be too shy, though, wouldn't you?"

She looked to him for encouragement. He made a face of mock alarm, raising his arms as if to ward her off. "Tell me more about Duke's office," he said.

"Well, the rug, for instance. Once I'd stepped on it I honestly wondered if I'd get my feet out. The pile was so deep that I couldn't even see my shoes. It was like standing in a field."

Daniel laughed.

"Also, a chandelier hung with ten thousand crystals dazzled me from above, and all I could think of was Lee, who saved her pennies for weeks on end to buy one crystal for her bedroom window, to catch the morning sun and make a color display on her wall. Not that her one crystal isn't more sublime and more loved than Duke's display, but it just staggered me. I felt a kind of fury that I've never known. And the receptionist must have come from Central Casting, and the secretaries—plural, mind you—too. It was revolting. I felt revolted."

"It's all tax-deductible, of course."

"Oh yes, he was quick to tell me that."

"Was he surprised to see you?"

"Very."


"Augusta. My goodness. What brings you here?" He drew her into his private office: desk, chairs, couch, and bar all furnished in leather and teak. Bay view furnished in glass. More plants. Eclectic artwork—eclectic was too nice a word. Mishmash would be better, Augusta thought. God, he could at least have asked my advice on the artwork.

But she made no comment on anything, only letting it give her strength to say brusquely, "I'm off to Oahu for the weekend . . . "

"Sure you are," he replied in his inimitable way that simultaneously threw her off and put her down. "Would you like a drink? This is all tax-deductible, by the way," he explained cavalierly, waving his hands at it.

She ignored his words and went on as if she had not been interrupted. " . . . so I've just stopped by to say aloha. I've arranged it all with the girls. No, thanks, I do not want a drink." He was standing with the bottle (Chivas) raised interrogatively. "I don't drink hard liquor anymore. Perhaps you haven't noticed. I haven't had a drink since last March. That's more than three months."

"What's all this about Hawaii? Sit down and tell me what's on your mind. Obviously you're overwrought about something. It's all this running. It's bad for you. You look awful."

Augusta glanced in the mirror by the door to assure herself that this was a lie. I've never looked better in my life, she thought. It's just that when I'm with him I get a drawn and wasted look. Also, he just says I look awful because he wants to. He doesn't really look at me any more than he listens to me.

"Duke, I am going to Honolulu. I am going to write the Third International Jogging Route for my book. I will return home Monday, but only for a little while, for I will have to make a long trip for the rest of the book. A *very* long trip."

He took a sip of his drink and looked at her quizzically, beginning to believe her, which softened her up.

"I am serious, Duke," she said sincerely, her voice trembling a little. "You haven't wanted to believe that I am serious about this book, but now you have to see that I am. I am serious about it and my running. It's something I really want to do and that I am going to do, and if you can't give me your support, which I wish with all my heart you would, then I'll have to do it alone."

"Where did you get the money for this trip?"

"Oh, Duke, how happy I would have been if you'd said anything but that. Anything!" Tears came to her eyes.

"How happy *I* would be if you'd answer the question."

"I borrowed it," she said bitterly. "I borrowed it." She turned away from him. "Good-bye. I'll see you Monday. But I wish I didn't have to. I wish I could just keep going. If it wasn't for the girls, I would."

As she struggled through the rug to the elevator, she felt awful about the way the interview had gone. But as the elevator door closed behind her, she experienced a revulsion of feeling and thought, with a rush of exaltation, *I'm going!*

Duke looked after her thoughtfully. After a moment he pressed a recording device on his desk and began: "To Ralph Cogan, Cogan, Cogan, and Ravenswing, 30 Charles Street, Boston, Massachusetts. Dear Sir, I am writing to inquire about the estate of the late Miss Hester Adams which my wife, Augusta Adams Gray, is heir to. It was my understanding that her will would have been probated by now and that the securities . . . "

# 10

..... *The Connection*

BANG!

At the sound of the gun, Ephraim saw Augusta jump and then begin to run like hell. But he was unable to go after her. It was a handicap race—and the women went out first.

Having scored zero on trying to find her in hotels or on Waikiki, he'd come looking for her in Kapiolani Park. He found her at the start of a race that was to go around Diamond Head to the Aloha Tower—eight miles. Now, if he was not to lose her, he must run the race too, and run it fast; Augusta had ten minutes on him.

*188. . .*

When the gun went off for the men's open division, Ephraim took the lead. It was a beautiful day: clear skies, temperature seventy-five, air soft and scented. Coming from the drought-stricken tip of the mainland, the greensward of Kapiolani knocked his eyes out. He felt full of energy as he started up the shoulder of Diamond Head.

It was half an hour before he caught sight of Augusta. She was in front! Bounding along like a gazelle. He was going too fast and was unable to check himself, so he drew abreast of her. She turned her face to him. Her skin was flushed red and wet from the heat and running. Her eyes gleamed with excitement, flashing brighter as she saw who he was, but not looking surprised. She smiled happily at him and looked as if she would speak, but didn't, couldn't, and so turned face front again to concentrate on the running.

Then an extraordinary thing happened. Ephraim felt himself locked into Augusta's stride and pace. His stride shortened slightly to adjust to hers. His pace subsided, but it was still amazingly fast. Together they sprang up off their left legs, soared through the air, landed on their right legs to spring off them and up and down. The colors of sea and trees and flowers moved by them in a rainbow blur as the road unraveled beneath their four feet. They breathed together, deep breaths in and out together, hearing the breaths as one breathing. Imperceptibly their bodies moved closer and closer until their arms, moving oppositely, brushed delicately with each stride. Taking a sudden turn, they moved as one person: turning, leaning into the curve, straightening. They were synchronized. They were one rapidly moving, deeply breathing organism, bioentrained. Ephraim felt that if he had wanted to ease up or move forward, he would not have been able to, so bound to each other were they. It was a powerful sensation—his first experience of intimacy. He recognized it as such, and yet the sensation was so primitive that *intimacy* seemed too civilized a word. He felt as if some deep tribal memory had emerged from his collective unconscious, harkening back to man's time as hunter and gatherer, and that the sound of their pounding feet and gasping breaths was a resonance from prehistory.

Augusta was experiencing the same sensual and emotional force of their deep connection. At the same time, she seriously doubted whether the man running beside her—as part of her—existed. Turning and seeing him there beside her, she was not surprised, because she had seen him so often in the last week. It seemed entirely plausible that he would be here in Hawaii with her as well—especially if he was a creature of her imagination. Did he have substance? Was he a hologram of her wildest dreams? A ghost, a fantasy, a hallucination, a conjuring, an angel? What was he? Who was he?

*What was happening to her?*

One thing that was happening was that she was running faster than she could possibly run. She could not run this fast. They were out in front of hundreds of people. Maybe he could run this fast, but she could not. She was only a woman, and not a young one. She was thirty-seven years old, and fast for her age and sex, but not this fast. He was pulling her along somehow, giving

her a strength and fleetness not her own. She was sub-
sumed into him. It wasn't just that *he* wasn't real; they
were *both* a fantasy, a vision of two long, lean, rapidly
running redheads on a tropical island moving along together faster than was humanly possible. Or maybe she
wasn't here, and it was only he who was the front-
runner, and she was him, gloriously transmogrified.

That's it! I'm not really here in body. *I am in his body!*

No. No such luck. A stabbing pain under her ribs
stunned her into reality, reminding her that she could no
longer exceed her possibilities for strength, speed, and
endurance without her body shattering into a million
pieces. By some miracle she had gone beyond her limits,
way beyond them, but now her body was crying out for
self-preservation, telling her in no uncertain terms that
she must stop or die.

It broke her heart to relinquish the race, to relinquish
these most thrilling moments of her entire life, but she
had no choice. The pain was everywhere now. But he
could go on. He could go on, and they would win.

Ephraim sensed her failure as soon as it began to happen. He turned to her and could see her trying to speak,
trying to find the breath to speak. Finally the words
came in a thin, whispery gasp that wafted across to his
ear. "Can't go on. Cramped. You go. Win. It's your race.
You've got it."

Then she fell away from him, was gone, and he was
running on. Her words gave him a leap of new energy so
that he accelerated, opening up the space between him
and the footsteps behind. He emptied his mind. He ran.
He felt full of running for its own sake. No thoughts now

of what it could *do* for him. He ran the road under. It disappeared beneath his feet as if his soles were drinking it. He imbibed the miles so that behind him there was nothing left, no one, no place, no time.

He saw the Aloha Tower ahead. That was the finish of the race. The race! He had run a race. For sport. And he had won it. He broke the tape. There were cheers and smiles. So many cheers and smiles. People were clapping him on the back and showering him with compliments. Other runners, finishing, surrounded him and spoke with enthusiasm and camaraderie.

"Hey, man, good race."

"I couldn't get near you."

"Kept thinking I'd take you on the homestretch. No way."

"Man, you were flying."

"Where are you from?"

"Have some Primo."

The cold beer washed down his throat. It was delicious. He'd never tasted anything so good in all his life. Someone put a trophy in his hand, announced his time. More cheers.

Ephraim was smiling. He felt . . . what did he feel? Good. Really good. But he'd felt good before. This was different, a new dimension of good feeling. It hadn't to do with the actual winning. It was everything else: the people, the smiles and words, the taste of the beer, the blue sky, the happiness of it all. That was it. He felt happy as all hell.

But what about Augusta?

Poor Augusta, moving to the side of the road so as not

to get trampled, fell dizzily down but stayed in a sitting position so as not to alarm anyone. Many runners called out to her as they ran by, "Are you all right? Do you need help?" Runners, she thought, are the nicest people in the whole world, a divine breed of gorgeous, healthy, glowing, kindly people.

She smiled and waved them all on. She was all right. It was just the unaccustomed heat and the incredible speed. Wow. Her brain was really turning around. No lovely euphoria this time—more like dementia. If Duke could see her now, what an orgy of I-told-you-so's he could have. But it still beat the hell out of an agoraphobic seizure. She'd rather be sitting at the side of a strange road in a strange place, momentarily weakened in mind and body, having run five fantastic miles, than be passed out on the seat of the hated Mercedes after a panicky fifty-foot flight from the library.

She got to her feet. I'm strong. I'm well. I'm happy. And what a runner I am!

No matter that as she thought this she was hobbling gimpily along feeling as though her body had sustained stress fractures, torn ligaments, unstrung hamstrings, incipient cases of tendonitis, and muscles pulled like taffy. No matter! That was par for the course. She would hitch a ride when she got to Ala Moana, Hono's main drag, and be in a heavenly hot tub before the hour was up. And after that, where was it written that she couldn't break training and have one of those fabulous rum Mai Tai drinks with an orchid floating in it that women carried around Waikiki just as women in San Francisco carried handbags?

So, within two hours, Augusta was happily ensconced

in the Banyan Court of the old Moana Hotel on Waikiki, in a tiny brown bikini, sipping a Mai Tai, and drafting her Third International Jogging Route.

# 11

..... *The Third*
*International Jogging*
*Route*

I WISH I could suggest to you a jog along Waikiki, but in all conscience I can't. There are simply too many impediments to a smooth jog. It is not a wide beach, and it is extremely busy. There are catamarans and canoes roaring up onto the sand on every ninth wave. There are obstructions like seawalls and fences and roped-off areas that you would have to stop and get over, and there are innumerable people doing all the things that people do on beaches: throwing balls and frisbees, lying spread-eagled covered with cocoa butter, creating pornographic sand sculptures, eating, drinking, flirting, and some of them even going in and out of the water. But it isn't just the business of the people that would impede you; it is their variousness, for you will want to stop and stare at them—the Japanese, for instance. If you have come from St. Paul, Minnesota, and have never seen an almost naked Japanese person, you will be so interested to discover that they are not yellow. Nor are they brown. Their skin is white, much paler, I would say, per capita than a Caucasian's, and much more flawless (which is to say no moles, freckles, wens, boils, or rashes). In essence, a dermatologist's despair. Also, their bodies— which are slim and sinewy—seem to be two-dimensional instead of three, so that if they turn sideways they disappear entirely. Unlike the Hawaiians, who are still prized for their fat and sideways are even more momentous.

Momentous? Augusta wondered. Do I mean momentous? And what about the jogging route?

I would like to say something about those tatooed Japanese gentlemen, though, she thought, looking at a table nearby. Let's see, I'd have to go back to where I'm talking about skin. Those really are the most elaborate tatoos I've ever seen on bodies.

She remembered a lithograph by Kenjila Nanao of three Japanese men with a serpent tatoo continuing along their three bodies. There must be a tatoo tradition in Japan, she thought, that Hiroshige didn't tell me about. Too bad we Americans have such a tatoo taboo.

Augusta laughed to herself. She felt so good. It was terrible that they had to return tonight just when she was getting into the swing of it all.

Friday they had been tired when they arrived. Saturday she'd had a nice relaxing day on the beach, but

Daniel had been busy with family and funeral arrangements, and she'd felt rather lonely and self-conscious going about by herself. She kept looking around for a daughter or two, for whenever she'd traveled before, the whole family had gone together. Duke had always looked after them and planned their days very carefully. It was strange to be totally alone. And the nights were difficult.

Friday night she awakened very frightened and disoriented, not knowing where she was or with whom.

She woke up, sat bolt upright in bed. Nothing was familiar to her. None of the shadowy forms were the right shape or in the right place in the room. The location of the bed in the general room plan was totally wrong. The slight light from the windows was not the right light. The darkness of the corners was a different darkness. It was all strange and unaccountable. She felt quite certain it was not her bedroom in Mill Valley.

Where am I? she wondered, heart pounding. Who am I?

She got up and groped around the room, bumping into things, trying to find the light switch. She opened a door and walked into horribly jangling hangers. She backed out and crashed into the bedside table.

"Ow!"

"Augusta!" Daniel turned on the light. "Are you sleepwalking?"

"Oh! Oh, Daniel, it's you. I was lost. I didn't know where I was. I'm in Hawaii, aren't I? With you. It's unbelievable."

She crawled back into bed. "Will you hold me tight for a minute?"

"Gladly."

The next night the same thing happened: the waking, groping, opening doors, culminating this time in upsetting the TV set so it fell against the wall and thence to the floor with an extremely loud concussion.

"Augusta? Again?"

Daniel was tired from a long and difficult day. His body was exhausted, and his patience was too.

"Daniel? Is that you?"

"No, it's Al Capone."

"Daniel, please hold me for a little while. I feel scared and sad and weepy. Will you?"

But by the time she crawled into bed he was asleep again. She put his arms around her as best she could, stifling the wild and desperate desire to call her children on the telephone.

But today, she thought as she sat under the fabulous banyan tree, has been wonderful. The race and now this, and soon Daniel will be back from the funeral.

Once again she addressed herself to the jogging route. She thought a minute, picked up her Pilot Fineliner, and wrote on.

> So, abandoning the idea of a jog on Waikiki, rise instead, early in the morning, not later than dawn, to avoid the heat, . . .

Augusta paused and reread her sentence. There seemed to be a hopeless syntax problem. It sounded like she was telling the reader to rise instead of jog. The Third International Rising Route, she thought, a guide to Honolulu levitation. She laughed aloud.

"How many Mai Tais is this?" Daniel was standing before her. He wore tan slacks and an open-necked white shirt. He looked blonder and browner than on the mainland, his hair curlier from the humidity.

"Only one. I'm just feeling so happy. This is the life! Was it a nice funeral?"

"Very nice. How was your race?"

"Wonderful. And now I am writing my jogging route. Would you say that this banyan tree is momentous?"

"Absolutely. Do you know that Robert Louis Stevenson sat under this very banyan tree to write his stories?"

"Yes, I do. That's why I'm sitting here to write. Good vibrations. I'm discovering that it's terribly hard to write even one good sentence, let alone an entire book. Daniel, would you like to go to our room and make love? It would be a very life-affirming thing to do after the funeral."

"Good idea. It makes me feel very, uh, momentous."

Augusta laughed, put on her robe, and gathered her things together. As they went into the hotel, he observed her and said, "Do you know that you're walking like an old, old woman?"

"I know." She told him more about the race and the pain, but she did not tell him about the redheaded man. She wanted to, but it was impossible. How do you speak the ineffable?

But I don't want to start keeping things from Daniel as I did from Duke, she thought, feeling slightly panicked. Later, she resolved, I'll give the ineffable a go. Later for sure. Maybe when she had thought about it some more, she could tell about it. But even then, it had been such an amazing experience that she feared to tell about it would be to lose it.

And Daniel, well, he wouldn't mock her as Duke would, but neither would he be moved or impressed. Nothing impressed Daniel, she realized, which was impressive in itself in a way, but also sad. She didn't like to admit it, but Daniel was rather jaded.

"Did you feel at all sad at the funeral?" she asked him as they went down the corridor to their room.

"No, she was really gaga these last years."

"But you must remember how she was when she was young, when you were little."

"I remember very well. When I was little she beat me regularly."

"Oh." Augusta thought about this. "Maybe," she said a few minutes later as they turned down the bed, "that turned you against women a little, on a certain dimension."

"Women are great to visit, but I wouldn't want to live with one."

"You really say such terrible things, but you say them in such a gentle, humorous way that I can't get mad at you."

"I don't let any woman get mad at me for fear she might beat me."

"That could be true, you know." Augusta looked at him searchingly.

"It's absolutely true. That's why I said it." He spread out his arms to her. "Shall we?"

"Let's."

# PART THREE

# 1

..... *Ephraim Reports*

EVALYN and Nancy were having Monday morning tea in
the suite when Ephraim called from the lobby.

Evalyn put down the phone. "He's back from Honolulu and on his way up in the elevator. Now we will
hear how he dispatched the sweat-suited one. I hope
there will be lots of gory details. I hope he got her on
the first night so they couldn't spend it together. One
thing I did discover, though. Daniel's mother truly did
die, so at least the weekend wasn't a hoax. Still, it is
quite unforgivable that he would take her with him.

Sometimes I think killing her isn't enough. He should be punished in some way as well. But I will have years to think about how after we are married."

"You still don't even know for certain that she did go to Hawaii with him."

"I know what I know. Am I ever wrong?"

"No."

"How did I become a multimillionaire?"

"By never being wrong."

"Then how dare you say I don't know something?"

"Sorry. I wasn't thinking. It just slipped out."

"I pay you to think. I pay you not to let things slip out."

"I'll never do it again. There's his knock." Nancy struggled out of her chair. She had to rebound off the back of the chair three times before getting enough momentum to rise to her feet, but once up she moved magnificently across the room and around the corner to the door.

Evalyn shouted after her, "I hate it when you say things like 'I'll never do it again.' You're so obviously trying to mollify me, and it's a patent falsehood."

"Patent pending," said Nancy meaninglessly, and quickly opened the door to Ephraim so that Evalyn would forget about her.

He wore a cream-colored shirt and matching pants with a dark brown suede jacket. He looked very well on the leopard rug, Evalyn thought as he gracefully crossed over it and stood before her.

"You wanted me to report to you as soon as I returned."

"Yes, indeed. Will you have tea?"

"Thank you."

"You will?"

"Yes, I like tea. No sugar or lemon."

"I somehow never think of you eating or drinking, Mr. Johnstone. I always imagine you survive on something planktonish, something you just inhale for a moment when you open your mouth to speak." She passed him his tea. "Nancy has just been accusing me of being wrong about this woman going to Hawaii. Was I wrong?"

"No."

Evalyn shot Nancy a scathing glance.

"So, you found her, I trust, even thought I was unable to tell you where they were staying. Daniel promised to call but didn't."

"I found her."

"Where?"

"Kapiolani Park. She had gone there to run."

"Excellent. And there the authorities found her the next day, I hope, under a bush, horribly mutilated."

"No."

"Very well. I'll let you tell the story yourself. You saw her in Kapiolani Park, and then what did you do?"

Ephraim went to the window, glanced out at the panoramic view, then looked at Evalyn. "I ran a race with her," he said.

There was a stunned silence broken by a small cough from Ephraim. He was coughing to clear his throat of a laugh. He covered his mouth and coughed again. Evalyn stared at him, apparently at a loss for words—a unique experience for her. Before he told them about the race, he'd had no idea how funny it would sound. But now he'd said it, he decided to let it stand and not elaborate. He liked it.

Evalyn carefully put her cup in the saucer and set the cup and saucer on the table. She turned to Nancy. "Did he say he ran a race with her?"

Nancy's face was turning red, as if she too might have a throat problem.

"It seems that at great expense I have sent an assassin to Hawaii to take care of a certain sweat-suited person, but instead of killing her, he ran a race with her. Surely not. No, he could not have said that. He must have said *erased*, and it sounded like *raced*." She turned wondering eyes to Nancy. "Surely he effaced her, Nancy, for that is what I have paid him to do. That was vewee bad of him not to kill the naughty girl. Me am vewee mad."

Ephraim widened his eyes at this new pattern of speech from Evalyn. "My intention," he said, "was to find her so that I could follow her to Daniel. I still have never seen them together. It is all assumption that she is the one. You understand that I do not wish to kill the wrong person."

"The fact that she was in Hawaii this weekend, added to the fact that you have seen her go into his building in San Francisco, weighs heavily in the direction of her being the person." Evalyn was sarcastic. "That would seem to me to be pretty goddamn proof positive."

"It does seem so," he said aloofly, almost sounding bored. "But *seeming* is not enough."

Evalyn got up and paced angrily back and forth, her robe whipping about at each turn. She was furious at the tone he had taken with her. "And you still don't know if she's the one, do you? You lost her, didn't you? You did not tail her to Daniel. Does it strike you that you are falling down on your job," she hissed at him, "that you are in fact falling apart, Mr. Johnstone? Does it? I saw you start to laugh a minute ago. For you that was comparable to another person having all-out hysterics. You are losing control."

Ephraim drew himself up imperceptibly, and it was apparent by this slight movement that he was now equally as angry as the frenziedly pacing Evalyn.

"I am going now for the tape," he said. "If she came back from the airport with him last night, her voice will be on it. Then I will have the proof that I require. Then and only then will I act."

"Excellent," she sneered. "But I am going to make a prediction, Mr. Johnstone. You will get the tape and their voices will be on it. You will act. You will shoot. And you will miss. You are never going to kill that woman. She has got to you somehow. God knows how. God knows how anybody could get to a cold fish like yourself—a cold, plankton-eating fish—but she has."

Ephraim relaxed. He saw that she was baiting him. (Since he was a fish?) Ephraim felt tempted to laugh again, to have "all-out hysterics" again. She was right. Laughing was losing control: laughing, crying, hitting. But he was all right. He would soon show how all right he was.

"Am I right?" she was asking. "Well, am I?

"Are you telling me you don't wish me to go on with the contract?"

"No, I am not," she shouted, articulating each word. "I am telling you to get on with it. I am at my wit's end."

She exited to the bedroom, slamming the door behind her.

Nancy mopped her brow. "Phew, what a scene." She looked curiously at Ephraim. "Why on earth did you tell her you'd run a race with the woman?"

"It just slipped out."

Nancy nodded. "I know what you mean." She was thoughtful. "Of course, I see what you mean, too, about not having the proof. This whole thing could be entirely supposition. Daniel may not have another woman. And if he does, it may not be this woman, who may have gone to Hawaii just to run the race. But there's no telling Evalyn that. She's convinced that she's never wrong. If she gets an idea in her head, she believes it only came there because of its rightness, and so she acts on it. In fact, she hired you before she even knew of the woman's existence! She hired you to kill an idea she had got in her mind."

Ephraim went to the door and opened it.

Nancy asked, "Do *you* think this running woman is the one?"

"Yes," Ephraim said, and closed the door behind him.

# 2

. . . . . *The Tape*

Daniel and Augusta got home Sunday night. She slept at his apartment, leaving Monday around noon.

Ephraim went from the Fairmont to Vallejo Street, saw Augusta leave, then Daniel. He picked the lock, went into the apartment, and secured the tape. When he got back to Strawberry Point, he put the tape in his stereo and the voices spoke at once.

"I just can't bear the thought of going home, Daniel. I feel I've made my break, and our weekend was so wonderful. I didn't want to tell you in Hawaii, but I've got

terrible troubles and I don't want to go home and face up
to them."

"If I'm going to hear troubles, I'd better pour myself a
drink."

"You drink too much, I think. It's not good for you."

"Listen, Scotch is about the only thing left that doesn't
contain carcinogens. Do you want anything?"

"Tea. I'll make it."

"Well, tell me all about it now that I'm fortified."

"It's all sort of a jumble. First of all, that red-haired
man?"

"The one who saved you from a watery death?"

"Yes. I see him everywhere. I think he's following
me."

"Maybe he's developed a passion for you."

"But whenever I try to speak to him—wave and smile,
show some recognition—he doesn't seem to see me. No,
I think he's following me. Maybe he was after me that
day at the cove as well."

"Duke's doing. I was afraid this would happen. It's the
divorce courts for Daniel, for sure."

"It could be your friend, the fabulous rich woman,
Evalyn."

"In that case I'd be followed, not you."

"Unless she's trying to find out who I am. But I feel as
though he's following me to protect me, not harm me. I
don't know; it's all so strange. But there has to be some
sort of deep connection established between two people
when one has saved the life of the other. It's heavy. The
thing is, he's too impressive-looking to be a simple detec-
tive hired to tail a promiscuous woman. He's too

interesting-looking. In fact, he's one of the most sensational-looking men I've ever seen. I think he is the Angel of Life."

"If you think he's so great-looking, maybe you're the one following him."

"No, but I think I will. I think I will follow him, Daniel, and find out who he is. I'll just go to his house and confront him. I do want to thank him for his gift of life, but now I'm feeling awfully curious about him as well."

"That sounds like a bad idea to me, lady. Leave it alone."

"Are you jealous?"

"No, nervous. I don't want anything to happen to you."

"You see? You really do care for me more than you realize. Right now, if you had to choose between me and Evalyn and there was no sea to escape to, whom would you choose?"

"Evalyn."

"You're just terrible."

"But I'd still go to your funeral."

"Now you've turned your only commitment to me into a joke—and not an amusing one."

"Sorry. Tell me more about your troubles."

"The other things is, at one point I told Duke I'd been running in the city, and I guess he thought about that, because he asked me later how I got to the city. He said he'd seen me in a blue sports car."

"I don't understand the problem."

"Oh, well, you see . . . he doesn't know I have my own car."

"Why not?"

"Well, I bought it secretly. I'd always wanted one and I just hated that big tank of an old Mercedes and the bus strike came and Duke kept taking the car and I had no way to get around . . ."

"Those are all good reasons. Why didn't you tell him some of them?"

"He would never have given me the money, and I didn't want him to know I had my own money. Not then, anyhow. It sounds rather awful. It's hard now to understand the state of mind I was in, but you see, I inherited some money, and I didn't want Duke to know I'd received it. I wanted to carry out my own plans, one of which was buying my own car. The money all came to me in stocks, and I sold all but two. This was back in May."

"The stock market's gone up since then."

"I know."

"Did you reinvest it?"

"Not really."

"Put it in a sock under your mattress?"

"Uh, sort of. It all began with the idea of the jogging book. I got this idea, which I've mentioned to you, and I determined to do it. At the time I really wanted to do it with Duke and transform our marriage, make him healthy and nice. We would do it together and become partners and boon companions, as I believed—still believe—a man and wife can be. He carped and said we couldn't afford to take a year off. But I knew we could with my money."

"He'd still have to leave his job."

"Yes, but he complains about his job all the time, and I thought he'd be glad of the chance to get away from it."

"All men complain about their jobs; it doesn't mean they don't like their work—especially when they do it well. They like the power that goes with it, the money, the challenge, the fascination. Or something in their nature is pleased by it. Still, a guy likes to complain. That's part of the drill."

"Still, wouldn't you leap at the chance to go around the world with me if I paid for it and . . . "

"Augusta, I'm afraid you're just not very realistic. Not only would it cost a lot of money, but he wouldn't be earning money during that time, so you can add those tens of thousands lost to the tens being spent, and the whole thing becomes unfeasible. And who's to say his job would be waiting for him upon his return?"

"But the book would make money, you see. And even if it didn't . . . I *hate* all this talk of money. Money isn't the only thing in life. What about a good marriage? Health, happiness, food for the soul, adventure, education! Why not look on inherited money as a bonanza with which to expand your life, transform your life! It just makes me sick. Daniel, you don't really mean it, do you? I mean, you are trying to show the sensible side, but you don't like money all that much. You see how much more there is to life. You believe in poetry, adventure. I know you do. You like to joke about Evalyn and her wealth, but I know it isn't important to you, or you wouldn't be fooling around with me. You would be doing everything to please her . . . "

The tape was finished. Ephraim shut off the machine. So, she was going to follow him, was she? He wouldn't put it past her. He wouldn't be surprised if she was at his apartment house door this minute.

He removed the tiny tape from his machine and pocketed it. He stood up, turned, and his heart jumped. Augusta was standing in his bedroom door.

"I don't believe it," he said

"I don't understand," she said simultaneously.

# 3

..... *Daniel Musing*

WHILE Augusta was confronting Ephraim at Strawberry Point, Daniel, disturbed in mind, was walking through the North Beach section of San Francisco, taking the air.

He was worried about Augusta. Despite his intention to keep it a casual affair, it was not casual as far as she was concerned, and he did feel responsible for her in part, if only because he liked her.

She was obviously not an old hand at love affairs, and although he'd been extremely careful and had tried to inculcate her with the fine art of sneaking around, she must have fallen down somewhere, so that Duke was alerted—and it just wasn't worth destroying a good long marriage over someone as unimportant as himself. But maybe Duke didn't know. If not, the redheaded man was Evalyn's agent. In which case it was up to him to do something about the problem.

Despite himself, Daniel's mind escaped to thoughts of the sea. Soon he would set sail again, and there would be the clean blue expanse of ocean and sky. The sunsets, the bustle of wharves, the satisfying order of watches, the taking on and putting off of pilots as they came into the various islands that appeared, blindingly bright and alive with color, sound, and action, after the daily scrutiny of the horizon line, the inexorable rhythm of waves. Then, once in port, he could swap tales in his cabin with South Sea traders and captains, with cold Australian beer as an antidote to the tropical heat ashore.

There were problems too: steering clear of coral reefs, storms, and passengers; living in close quarters with the same men for weeks on end; stevadores deciding to strike when the cargo was half loaded on the ship. But for the most part, the ocean was where he was happiest and most involved. He had been too long ashore and had broken a cardinal rule of keeping his relationships light. Broken it not with one woman but with two.

He respected them both: Evalyn for her power, wealth, and intelligence; Augusta for her sweetness, joy of life, pussy.

It occurred to him that if the redheaded man was Evalyn's agent, the best thing to do was to mention Augusta to her and play down her position in his life, even make up some story about her being a relative—an odd relation, very odd. But if Evalyn did not know about Augusta it would certainly be a shame to bring her up.

Evalyn struck him as a very possessive woman. Look at Nancy, whom she didn't allow any personal life. Yes, look at Nancy O'Hara. Every time Daniel did look at her, he had second thoughts about continuing with Evalyn, felt his stomach for signs of added girth, found them. He certainly tended to eat and drink more with Evalyn; he didn't know exactly why. Maybe simply because it was such good grub. She could always afford the best. Indeed. But it was he who paid the bill. Dating a millionaire was expensive unless one thought of it as an investment toward marrying her. Honestly, how could he throw away fifteen mil?

Daniel sighed. He'd be a fool not to marry her, a fool! Besides being rich, she was charming, interesting; he did respect her, and she doted on him. What was the problem? Well, look at Nancy O'Hara. Or look at something you sometimes saw in Evalyn's eyes. Or some things she sometimes let drop. Here was a woman who would stop at nothing, and he could not live easily with such a person. There were too many things he would stop at, multitudes. But rather than fight with her about them, he would probably take to food and drink, stuffing unsaid words back down his throat rather than make waves. He pictured himself and Nancy, two gross figures flanking the elegant Evalyn over the years, larding over their consciences with haute cuisine. Tweedledee and Tweedledum.

His mind began sliding off to sea again, but he hoisted

it back to the problem, which was essentially Augusta and the possibility of some sort of harm coming to her. If Evalyn was on the scent, she must be distracted. One solution would be to say he would marry her. Saying wasn't doing, after all, and saying would assure Evalyn of his, uh . . . commitment—to borrow a word from Augusta—his commitment to her and . . . oh, hell! Maybe he would just go down to the ship for an hour or so. It was in dry dock now, getting the grass and barnacles removed from its hull so they could gain a few knots on the next voyage. It would be nice to talk to some of the boys. Let's see. He looked at his bejeweled wonder-watch. Evalyn was picking him up at five. He had two lovely hours to mess with. He flagged a cab and directed the driver to the Oakland shipyard. He sat back.

"Women!" he sighed.

"I hear you," said the cabby.

# 4

. . . . . *Augusta Gray,*
*Nemesis*

EPHRAIM and Augusta stared at each other. Of the two,
Ephraim was the more off-balance. Augusta was upset,
angry, and bewildered. But Ephraim was frightened. It
was a deep, primeval fear such as one can only feel when
confronted with the inexplicable. It was dissociation, a
momentary feeling of not knowing who he was or where
he was. His mind went whirling away in a cosmic
maelstrom while his body stood apart watching it go off
without him, his nervous system signaling the darkest
fear of all—that he was losing his mind.

This had never happened to him before, but Augusta knew the fear well, so well that for a year she'd had to arrange her every action around it. And even now, with her phobic episodes behind her, she was often terrified because of the extreme life changes she was making. Breaking out of her homeostasis was as frightening as the most daring jailbreak where, despite high walls, barbed wire, searchlights, armed guards, and known informers, you were committed to the attempt. She knew what it was to wake in the night covered with sweat, a vision of the abyss all around her.

"I don't believe it," "I don't understand," they said simultaneously.

"How did you get in here?" Ephraim asked, staring at Augusta.

"You look so frightened. Why?"

"How . . . ?"

"And why do you have that tape? What are you going to do with it?"

"Answer *me*," he demanded. "How did you get in?"

"It seems we are both guilty of an invasion of privacy, but what you have done is unconscionable." Augusta felt hot and teary as more and more it was borne in upon her that her tender moments with Daniel had literally been stolen from her. That which should be forever ephemeral had been cruelly seized, fastened, and probably labeled, like butterflies transfixed under glass, nevermore to flutter in the air or to flash opalescent in the sunlight. Just as primitive people feel their souls can be stolen by a photographic portrait, so did Augusta feel that her soul had been violated by the tape.

"I will answer your question when you have answered mine," said Ephraim.

"I followed you in," Augusta said.

"That is impossible. Elaborate for me. I must know. I want to know."

He said this with such intensity, such sincerity, that Augusta felt a strange thrill. It was because no one had ever said "I want to know" to her before. It made her feel important to this man. Strangely, it made her feel cared for. She realized that someone wanting to know you, or to know about something you did, was a great deal more powerful, more moving, than someone wanting to have you.

But what to tell him? As usual, leaving Daniel's, she had been in one of her *states* whereby she went from pont A to point B without really giving any instructions to herself about it. Often she was surprised to find herself where she was without any clear memory of how she'd gotten there. No, not how, for she knew that she'd run there or driven there, but she didn't recollect details of passage. Nevertheless, feeling they had struck a bargain, she tried to give him a forthright account.

"After I left my friend's house, at around noon, I went to the John Berrgruen Gallery downtown to pick up an etching I had bought, and that must have taken me as long as it took you to steal into Daniel's for the tape after you had seen me safely out of sight. We met on the bridge returning to Mill Valley. You were several cars ahead of me, but of course I recognize your car by now, so I followed you to your building, up the stairs, and into your apartment. I simply"—she shrugged—"followed you. You were intent on hearing the tape right away, so you went directly to your stereo before you closed the door. I slipped in and would have spoken at once, but then I heard Daniel's voice issuing from your machine, and out of curiosity I decided to hear the thing out. I hid in your bedroom."

"Who is your teacher?"

"I beg your pardon?"

"Is it Morihei Uyeshiba?"

"No, but if I am to have a Japanese teacher, I guess it would be Hiroshige." She had to smile as she thought of her gentle old friend Hiroshige. What would he think of all this?

"There is no master of the martial arts by that name. Hiroshige was an artist of the *ukiyo-e* period."

Augusta was pleased that he knew this. "Yes! Nevertheless, he taught me to see, how to move and not to move, how to blend." She smiled and let her mind take off with the notion. "Now that I think of it and try to examine it, I believe I followed so closely behind you that I did in fact blend with you. Shadowing you, I became your shadow, became you, so that I entered your apartment subtly encased by you. Don't you think that is possible? Don't you think it happened in Hawaii?"

They were both silent. Embarassed, Augusta lowered her eyes as if she had referred to a night of love. She continued. "I feel that I know you so well. Before this shock of hearing the tape, I wanted so much to thank you for saving me and to tell you . . . that you are not responsible for me. I thought you were laboring under the ancient Chinese injunction that if you have saved someone's life you are responsible for them as long as they live. I thought you had taken on this responsibility to a weighty degree, following me everywhere as you did, and I wanted to free you. Now I see that I was probably foolish to think this. That was just one of my theories. Another one was that you are the Angel of Life. But that's really silly, isn't it? The Angel of Life does not make tapes."

Ephraim had been listening attentively. Now she waited for him to speak. But he didn't.

"Will you please tell me about the tape now?"

"No."

"But you said . . . "

"I lied. And you have not answered anything. You have been talking garbage. Hiroshige! This is no explanation. But the fact remains that you are here. Now I must decide what to do. Don't speak, please. Sit down and be completely quiet while I think."

Ephraim had recovered from his fear; his mind had returned to his skull. He was once again on balance, centered. He would puzzle out later how she got here. There must be an explanation. But not one that would excuse incredible negligence on his part. If she was telling the truth, he was finished. Or maybe he had simply met his nemesis, who, once destroyed, would release him from this debilitating ineptness. Yes! Ephraim took heart. Everyone had a nemesis, the one unconquerable opponent. He should go with it, be glad he'd met her early on, and rather than be cowed, go forth with a glad heart to this mystic engagement and scourge himself of her once and for all.

But isn't it inherent in the nature of a nemesis that she cannot be bested? Ephraim, looking at the woman sitting quietly on the couch—a woman no longer young, an ordinary person, a mother and faithless wife, a nonprofessional, a woman of no special merit physically or intellectually—did not see how she could be cast as a divine agent. Yet the facts were clear; she rendered him powerless. Her presence here in his apartment was proof.

Augusta sat quietly on the couch as he had told her to do. She still didn't know his name, but she could check it on the mailbox when she went out. If she went out. She had a slight, oppressive sense of imprisonment. But why? Who was he? What was all this about?

It was a nice apartment. She liked its emptiness. The masks were fine. She didn't know much about primitive art. She should address herself to it. That's really where art began, after all, not with Giotto. And it probably will end there, too, she thought sadly. After all, life on earth will end, and in the meantime my life will end. I wish it wouldn't.

"The thing is," she said, blurting out her thoughts, "if someone has gone to all this trouble to hire you to get the goods on me, then someone really cares about me, which is wonderful. I'd love to know. Does Duke? Does Duke love me? You want an explanation of how I came to be here, but where to begin? The day in the market, I suppose, when I first got the idea for an International Jogging Book. At that time I was an agoraphobic woman confined to her home and town, to her husband, daughters, and cherry tree. But I got an idea to write a running book, and so I started to run, believing it would strengthen my marriage. However, I found to my surprise that I was running off my phobia and running away from my marriage. I ran right into Daniel. Would I have turned like a sensually deprived person to Daniel if I felt loved by Duke? You have heard on the tape about the money. Does one have to practice deceptions if one is free? In a marriage that is a true partnership, does a woman behave as I have? Afraid of cars, buses, crowds, shops, I took to my heels. I ran away. I ran looking for love, friendship, support, understanding—and I found sex. Sex which is, I suppose, an illusion of all the foregoing. Daniel took me in his arms, gave sustenance to my poor starved body. But does Daniel love me? He says not, and I'm beginning to believe him. Still, if you are Evalyn's agent, it would appear that she *thinks* he loves me. But what will she do with the knowledge? If neither Duke nor Daniel loves me, then you have confused me with someone else or . . . Are you a CIA person, a G-man, a narc? I assure you that Daniel isn't a spy. He's so gentle, a nice man who doesn't want to be bothered. Don't bother him. I beg you not to harm him. Or maybe you're after Duke. Now, he could well be a Russian spy. Won't you speak to me?"

"No, and I must ask you again to be quiet while I think."

Augusta quietened, thinking, He will not tell me anything, I know that now. She turned her thoughts to the phlegmatic man across from her. As she had on the beach, she still felt pity or solicitude for him, a desire to heal him, to make him smile. That was still her gut reaction, though she was not sure why. He was not bleeding today. In fact, he looked totally bloodless. Usually a red-head's blood rages so close to his transparent skin that one can see it without cutting. But this man had tamed his blood long ago.

I had better tell Daniel about all this. It must have more to do with him than me. He must be advised, and all he wants now is his blessed sea.

And if Duke has hired this man? Then he will soon know all about Dan and me. Then what? I hate to think. Maybe he could take the girls from me on the strength of this.

That thought made her rise from her chair. "I'm going. If you will not explain about the tape, it's bootless for me to remain. As for your plans for it, I guess I'll just have to wait and be surprised." She grimaced and shrugged as if it was all unimportant. In a way it was. "I feel that whatever is destined to be for us will be, don't you?"

"Yes."

"So . . . I'm going." She paused at the door. She had somehow expected him to try and stop her; perhaps she wanted him to stop her.

"Shall I go?"

"Yes, go," he said.

She went. Ephraim went to the window, saw her sprint to her car, watched the car become a small blue spot on the black macadam.

He had to let her go. He could do nothing with her here. He could do nothing while she was close to him. He had resolved to hit her from a distance, and he saw more than ever that he must keep to that resolution if he was to succeed. He saw more than ever that he must succeed.

Ephraim fell into a brown study by the window, and almost trancelike, he went to his closet. He got his rifle down from the highest shelf. Disengaging the stock from the barrel, he placed it in a flight bag. He walked to his car, ignited the engine, and headed for the city, feeling sure that Augusta would go back to Daniel's to talk over this development. When he got to the end of Vallejo Street, he positioned himself on the roof of a building across from Daniel's, a place he had often used before. He fitted the rifle together, including the telephoto lens over the sights. He settled himself to wait indefinitely for Augusta to run up the hill or out of the building. This was it.

# 5

. . . . . *Violence*

AUGUSTA did not go directly to Daniel's; she went home so that she could call him and get his advice. She hoped the girls wouldn't be home. She leapt out of the car and went through the gate, under the branches of the cherry tree which were now thickly foliaged and full of birds. She patted the wrinkled old trunk that was like a petrified mastodon's leg. "I'm home," she said.

She went into the house, through the porch, the dining room, and kitchen, to her half-room. There, sitting on the single bed, looking through her papers, was Duke.

*228. . .*

"Duke!"

He turned to her with such a look of fury, of hatred, that she quailed. He knows, she realized. The red-haired man must have called. She felt frightened.

"You know?" she said stupidly.

"I know everything."

"Everything? That's . . . a lot." Her mind, like a caged bird, frantically flew to all the things there were for him to know. Strangely, the bird roosted on the Hiroshige. Could he know about that? she wondered. He is sitting on it now. I hope he hasn't broken the glass. The mattress was greatly indented by his weight.

"Yes, everything." He stood up, looking wild-eyed. It was hard to believe that this apoplectic man was her husband of many years, the father of her children. He seemed a stranger. Have I done this to him? Is this all my doing?

"Do you know what you've done?" He spoke from a throat so clenched that the words came out like blows.

"Yes, I know. I know everything." She laughed slightly hysterically. "It's so dumb. We keep saying the same thing—that we know everything. It's a relief, really. I'm *glad* you know and that I know . . . that you know." She laughed again.

At her laughter the blood rushed to his face. No tamed blood here. "I have just received a phone call. How could you have done this to me?"

"I had to," she said softly, feeling trembly. "I had to be my own self. My body is my own now, and my mind." She said the words like a litany. "I am Augusta. It is my life. I've harmed no one."

"You are a fool! You have harmed us all. It is a disaster. You are a stupid, irresponsible woman!"

"Why are you going through my papers? You have no right."

"I have every right," he shouted. "I am your husband. Aren't I? Aren't I?"

"No," she whispered. He wasn't listening.

"I have just talked to the executor."

"The executor. The red-haired man is an executor? What does he execute? I don't understand. And it was wicked of you to have us taped."

"For God's sake, don't start talking about the red-headed man. Him and running are all you've babbled about for weeks, and I have had it. I want straight talk from you, and I am asking the questions."

"Executor?"

"Sit down, Augusta." He grabbed for her, but she backed out of the room, truly scared now by the expression on his face. She ran.

She ran. Through the kitchen, through the dining room, onto the porch, through the front door, and down the path.

And Duke ran after her. Furiously he ran after her, shouting and gesticulating, demanding explanation, reparation; like a madman, a bereaved man, a man who has lost all, he shouted, running after Augusta.

But she could run very fast and he could not run at all, so she was in her car and away by the time he got to the cherry tree, where, breathing hard, he still shouted. "Exxon! General Motors! St. Regis. Forty dollars a share and going up. Up, Augusta. Now it's gone. Where?

Where is all the money? That car! You *do* have that sports car! What else have you bought? Come back!"

Augusta heard none of this, but the old people who lived on the quiet lane, deaf as almost all of them were, could hear Duke—see him, hear him, and feel alarmed for him. They tottered through their gates and came to help him. Old Lem, eighty, a retired county sheriff, still big and strong, was there to catch him in his arms when Duke's heart failed. His heart, unable to take this running and shouting, this rage and grief, attacked him, and he fell into old Lem's arms.

Lem's wife, because of a bad experience at the county hospital, summoned an ambulance from the city, and Augusta passed it on the bridge. She was speeding, hell-bent to get to Daniel. Toward what end she wasn't sure. Safety for herself? Warning for him? Would he protect her from Duke? Would he have her? Did he love her?

Augusta was extremely upset. She couldn't arrange her thoughts at all. She counted on Dan to help her. She would tell him everything. Which was what? Well, that the red-haired man had taped their voices because he was an executor. (?) That he (the executor) had telephoned Duke, who was now dangerously angry. That Duke had strongly believed himself to be her husband, but he wasn't. That she'd found him going through her papers. (Why was he going through her papers? For love letters? She wished there were some. Not for him to find, but for her to have.) How incriminating was the tape? She tried to run it through her mind and failed. Her mind was spinning. Why did Duke say she was not to talk about the red-haired man if he (Duke) now knew she knew? (?) Nothing made sense. Probably she should have tried to talk with Duke instead of running like a coward, but he'd forbidden her to babble. And he was so awful. She couldn't stand him anymore. She wanted to be with Daniel in the kindly comfort of his arms, soothed and cherished, not hated and shouted at and accused.

Ephraim waited on the roof of the building across from Daniel's, so still that some grackles landed there and pecked about near his feet without noticing him. At last he saw the little blue car coming up the hill. He raised his rifle.

Augusta drove right up to the very end of Vallejo Street, and after maneuvering around a huge, yellow, chauffer-driven Rolls-Royce that was parked proprietarily in front of Daniel's building, she parked illegally.

Ephraim lost her behind the Rolls-Royce.

As Augusta got out of her car, Daniel got into the Rolls. Augusta ran over to the Rolls, to the door he had entered, and banged on the window.

"Daniel!"

He didn't respond. She pressed her face against the window and looked in. He was leaning way over as if looking for something on the floor of the car.

"Daniel?"

Ephraim watched through the telephoto lens. He saw the Rolls begin to move and waited for its passage to reveal Augusta.

Augusta was moving with it, still looking in the window. Daniel was still searching for something on the floor of the car. She called to him. "Daniel. Help. I need you." She knew there was no way he couldn't hear her. Also, he must have seen her car drive up as he was coming out of his building.

Inside the car, Evalyn spoke drily to Daniel. "Darling, there is a woman trying to get your attention—banging, in fact, on your window, and shouting that she needs you."

"Oh."

"Are you hiding from her and pretending the glass is soundproof?"

"Yes."

"Well, she sees you perfectly clearly, though you are crouched in that ridiculous way. It might have appeared at first that you had dropped something on the floor, but any fool would understand that you would have found it by now."

"Has she gone now?"

"No. She is running along beside the car."

"She would. She's a bit strange. Very odd. No one important in my life, you understand. Just an odd . . . er . . . relation who runs."

"Do you think she will keep running beside us for miles?"

"I wouldn't be surprised."

"Aurora, drive faster."

"There's a stop sign ahead," said Aurora.

"Run through it. We are trying to shake this person off our car."

Now Augusta realized that Daniel was hiding, and a

deep dismay took hold of her, a pain in her heart like a stone. She faltered. At the same time, she saw that there was a woman in the back seat of the car with Daniel and that this woman was looking at her much as Duke had done half an hour earlier—with hatred. "Do you know what you have done?" Duke had screamed.

Indeed, what had she done to incur such hatred—from him, from this woman—and to have her lover, Daniel, shun her in the end?

Daniel, straightening up from his extremely uncomfortable position, also saw the hatred in Evalyn's eyes as she looked out at Augusta. It terrified him.

Augusta heard "Drive on" and felt the car lunge forward. Dismayed, sick at heart, she slowed her steps. Her lover not only would not help her, he would not acknowledge her.

Augusta stopped running. The big yellow car surged on. Ephraim's rifle sights now contained the image of Augusta. There was a deafening explosion. It was the sound of another car at the cross street smashing against the very spot on the side of the Rolls where Augusta had been clinging only milliseconds before. Ephraim, distracted from his shot, raised his eye from the sights to see what had happened. Augusta was not reacting. He set his sights on her again, instantly pulled the trigger, and that was the instant she reacted. She sprinted down to the accident scene and got lost in a crowd of citizens and police who had already materialized out of nowhere. True to Evalyn's prognostication, Ephraim had missed.

# 6

*. . . . . In Hospital*

THE next day, Nancy O'Hara came to Children's Hospital to see Evalyn. As she entered the room she exclaimed, "Evalyn, my dear, your poor black eyes! I called this morning from Sacramento, and Clara told me about the accident. I came straightaway. Are you all right?"

"No, I'm not all right, and if you've brought me flowers I'll scream."

Her room was full of roses and dahlias, and the superabundance had crossed the fine line between gaiety and funerealness.

. . . 235

"Of course I haven't brought flowers. I brought Mumms, not chrysanthemums."

"Pour it out quickly. I'm having champagne withdrawal."

Nancy did so, and Evalyn opened her throat and poured the drink down like a Spaniard drinking from a *bota*. She swallowed the champagne in gulps from the second glass, and by the third glass she was able to sip the stuff in a leisurely way.

"I'm getting out of this crummy place tomorrow morning. My suite doesn't cost much more per day than all this, and at least at the Fairmont I get some comfort and service and quiet. All I need is rest so that my bruises can come to full flower and fade and so my mild concussion can mend." She smiled. "As for poor Daniel . . ."

"How is he?" Nancy asked absentmindedly. She was deliberating whether or not to sit down. If she did she'd have to get up continually to pour Evalyn's champagne, but if she moved the chair over . . . "Is he here too?" It was an awfully small chair.

"Yes, just down the hall. Collarbone, three ribs, and one leg broken. But he will be all right. I will have the Traders deliver his food. He's been moaning deliriously for the sea since he came out of anesthesia. But he shan't have his sea. We're engaged. Catching him at that vulnerable moment, I got him to agree that it's me he wants, not sea. I made him see, as it were, and he saw."

Which suggested an old nursery rhyme to Nancy: See-saw, Marjorie Daw, Daniel shall have a new master; he shall get but a penny a day because he can't work any faster. "Poor Daniel," she said aloud. "Because of his broken bones, I mean," she added hastily. "I congratulate you both on your engagement." She pulled the chair over near Evalyn's bed and sat down. Just as she'd suspected, it could not contain both buttocks. Oh, well, at least it took a load off her feet. "Tell me how it happened."

"It was all the fault of that mad running woman who was clinging to the car. In my anger, I told Aurora to run the stop sign and—blindly obedient bitch that she is—she did. For a minute I thought the car that came at us was our hired killer poised to hit the woman. It wasn't, but I would be interested to know why our master assassin hasn't dispatched her. It can't be good for his self-esteem. And here she ends by almost killing me and Daniel. Well, it doesn't matter now."

"Right," said Nancy. "It doesn't matter now. So why go on with it?"

"What?" Evalyn looked sharply at Nancy.

"Let the girl go."

"But then she'll have won."

"Won what? You've got Daniel, haven't you? *You've* won."

"But she has annoyed me, given me grief, landed me in the hospital. Why should she get off scot-free?"

"Because there's no longer any *reason* for her to die, Evalyn."

"I hate her. That's reason enough for me."

"You can't hate a person you don't even know. It's just an idea that you hate."

Evalyn looked at her narrowly. "Why does this matter so much to you? What do you care whether she lives or dies?"

"I've hated the whole idea right from the beginning, as you damn well know."

"So I'm to call it off to please you?"

"Well, it wouldn't hurt you to save the fifteen thousand dollars, either."

"That's true. Now, that's talking my language. Let me think a minute." Evalyn thought. "All right. Get me Mr. Johnstone on the phone.

"This is Evalyn Ruth speaking. I am canceling the contract. I am weary of the entire business. Daniel is in Children's Hospital with broken bones. I too am in the hospital, nursing bruises. We were in an auto accident, and I can only trust that it was not you who hit us. But nothing would surprise me now. Don't include me in your highest references in the future. The woman still runs rampant, but I don't feel threatened by her anymore. It no longer matters."

Replacing the receiver, Ephraim said to himself, I'm afraid it still matters very much to me. It is a matter, to me, of life and death.

He donned a beautiful deerskin jacket. Into its specially tailored inside pocket he slipped his specially designed pistol. On his bare desk he left instructions for the movers who were coming to pack, move, and store his furniture. He had made arrangements for the safekeeping of his masks, and his suitcases were in the trunk of his car. He had read over the draft of his new novel and decided to dump it. It was curiously boring.

He drove to Children's Hospital. Good of Evalyn to have told him where Daniel was, although he had already found out. He parked and stationed himself under a sycamore tree half a block up from the hospital entrance. Visiting hours were almost over. Augusta would be coming out soon.

In her hospital room, Evalyn put down the receiver after talking to Ephraim. She smiled. I have saved myself fifteen thousand dollars, she thought, tickled pink, and he will still finish the job, hoping to restore himself to his former perfection. And he will. This time he won't miss.

Nancy, meanwhile, had gone down the hospital hall to see Daniel. Confusing the numbers, she went into the wrong room and was glared at by a distinguished but ill-looking man. "Sorry, wrong room," she said.

It was Duke.

# 7

. . . . . *More Violence*

AUGUSTA, who arrived at the hospital when Nancy did, went right to Daniel's room.

At first he didn't recognize her. Slim, graceful, wearing a slinky brown dress, her long hair smooth and shining, she quietly entered his room. He'd never seen her in a dress.

"Augusta, go away."

"I just want to talk a minute. How are you?" She thought he looked pitiful. All the bad thoughts she'd worked up against him were dissipated at the sight of him. "Poor Daniel. Can I come in?"

"I'm helpless to stop you. Come in. Come in and tell me why you were running after Evalyn's car. Why? Why?"

"Because I thought that Duke had found out about us. I desperately wanted to talk to you. You hid from me. It wasn't very nice. Was it because Evalyn was there?"

"Yes."

"You could have made up some story about me."

"I did."

"I'd rather you had seen my distress and cared enough to . . . to own me, to say, 'Wait Evalyn, stop the car, I must speak to my friend who appears to be in trouble.' Instead you urged the car on."

"I'm a coward."

"The truth is, you don't love me, do you?"

"No, I don't, but you're a nice lady. Go home to your husband."

"I can't. He's not home. He's just down the hall. He had a heart attack. I thought it was because he found out about us, but really it was over the money. Imagine almost dying over money!"

"It happens every day."

"He'd written to the executor who called to tell him that the money—or the securities, rather—had been sent to me in May. Then Duke went through my desk and learned from the broker's statement that I'd sold the stocks. At which bad moment I arrived on the scene. So he had a heart attack. Not a bad one, thank God. I'd never have touched the stocks if I could have foreseen the outcome. His life is more important to me than any amount of money. But strangely, it isn't to him."

They were both quiet.

Daniel carefully shifted his position. "What about the redheaded man? What's become of him, or did it turn out you imagined him?"

"No, I went to his apartment. He had made a tape of our last visit together. I still don't know why. I thought he must be Duke's agent. Now I think it must be a case of mistaken identity. Unless he's in Evalyn's hire."

"If so, she'll let it alone now."

"I feel so sad. Maybe there is no such thing as love between man and woman. Maybe you're right. But I have my running. I am a runner now. I will simply go running around the world alone."

"Go back to your husband. You've had a good marriage. You've got two good kids."

"I thought it was a good marriage up until last March. Now, from here, it looks horrible. I can't go back to him now. I'm too changed. In mind and body. I love him. I care whether he lives or dies, but he must do whichever without me. And you? Will you marry Evalyn?"

"Yes."

"I wish you joy with all her money. I'm glad you told me. It makes it easier. It makes me think you really are a rat."

Daniel was silent.

"Good-bye, Daniel. Have a nice life. Thank you . . . for the rapture. I guess for you it was all pretty mechanical. But for me, it was my first rapture."

Daniel sighed. "Good-bye, Augusta."

As she left Daniel's room, a fat lady walked in. Augusta stared. She had never seen a woman so enormous, even in Hawaii. Hawaii. She could not believe she'd been there with Daniel two days ago, so happy. Now it was good-bye forever.

She went down the hall to Duke's room. On the way she encountered his doctor, who was also a friend, a Princeton man—as was Duke's lawyer, and as would be his barber and shoeshine boy if Princetonians ever stooped to such lowly professions.

"How's he doing?" she asked.

"Great. He's tough. He'll be okay—so long as he quits smoking."

"Thank God," she said sincerely. She walked on to his room.

When he saw her the blood mounted to his face in such a rush that she was afraid her presence might cause another attack.

"I'm just here to say good-bye," she said soothingly. "I'm going off around the world to write my running book."

"You're mad!"

"I shall go alone. I have made arrangements for the children. When you are released from here, perhaps you can get on one of the ships with your beloved fruit and take a convalescent voyage. We can talk about a divorce upon my return."

"You are not divorcing me, Augusta."

"Yes, I have to. I won't ask for alimony because I shall live on the proceeds from my International Jogging Book."

"You won't make one nickel from that book, and you will blow your whole fortune in the writing of it. You are crazy."

"Please don't arouse yourself. I know your feelings.

But it is my life, and although I am discouraged about some things, for the most part I feel full of hope. I feel that I am embarking on a great adventure and that through the vehicle of my book I can share my discoveries with others. I can encourage other lonely, fearful women to run out in the world and embrace life."

"Yeah, go ahead. Go ahead and encourage them to destroy their marriages, abandon their kids, and tell their husbands to fuck off after they've blown his money that he broke his ass for years to make. And be sure to tell them how to give him a heart attack, too. You don't want to leave out that goody. Why don't you have before-and-after pictures? Before: a lovely, gentle wife and mother, a happy husband. After: a gaunt, wild-eyed bitch and a hospitalized husband. Well, you're not getting one penny from me when you come crawling back. Not one penny!"

"It's funny," she remembered. "I had originally planned before-and-after pictures, but they were not to be like that."

She smiled at him. "As for your pennies, I don't want them, Duke, not one. It is so wonderful to think that I'll never have to talk about money with you again, never be dependent." She went to the door, turned, saw him looking so wounded. "I'm sorry, Duke," she said, seeing how sad it all was. "I loved you. I love you still. You've been a good husband, a loving father to the girls, but I can't live with you anymore."

"You always said we'd grow old together."

She was so moved by this that she almost went back into the room to him. "I know," she admitted.

It was such a beautiful image—two people growing old together, companions down through the years—and she knew she still had a dream of this, in spite of everything. But there were dreams and there was delusion, and her life with Duke had become a delusion. She did not want to grow old with Duke. Better to be alone than with someone intolerable. To be old and poor and alone was a mighty fear that governed people, and so they lived on with mates who had become repugnant to them. Augusta did not entertain this fear. She would leave Duke with a high heart and take whatever might come.

"Good-bye, Duke."

She turned and went. She went down the hall, down the elevator, and through the main door of the hospital.

Augusta went down the hospital steps. Tonight she would have a farewell dinner with her daughters and friends, then fly away that evening. In her pocketbook was seventeen thousand dollars in traveler's checks. At home, her bag was all packed with, among other raiment, a new light blue sweat suit and a beautiful pair of bright red Nike Waffle Trainers—for running over mountains, which she planned to do when she wearied of city pavements.

She felt sad to leave her girls and lonely at the prospect of going off by herself, but she knew she'd meet other runners. They would fall in beside her and run through bits of the world with her. They would find each other. They were a fraternity, a sorority, and they spoke a common language with their feet.

Augusta walked down the hospital steps and started down the block to her car.

There he was! Her heart pounded like one of Daniel's grammar school hearts. Seeing him, she knew that she'd expected him to be waiting for her. He stood in the shade of a tree near her car. She smiled and waved and walked happily toward him. Then something slammed into her chest, and pain exploded in her mind, ending her. I am ended, she thought. It is over, just when it was about to begin. But he was coming toward her. He would save her life again.

Ephraim saw Augusta come down the hospital steps and begin to approach him. He removed the safety catch and aimed the gun. He saw her see him, saw her wave and smile. He squeezed the trigger. She kept walking toward him, smiling. The bullet took so long. How slowly the bullet traveled, as if time had stopped. 'There is no time or space before Uyeshiba of *aikido*, only the universe as it is.' Augusta had stopped the bullet in time. He could still go after it, get it, move her aside before it hit her. No, too late. Too late. She had stopped the bullet in her body. The bullet hit her now and knocked her off her feet. The force of it had thrown her down. She was falling now, hit. He turned to drift away. He turned. . . . His mind urged him to turn. . . . But he did not turn. He was going toward her, not away. He was moving toward her, hurrying, running toward her, not away.

# 8

. . . . . *Waiting*

"THE red-haired man saved me. Tell them. Tell them what the emergency nurse said."

It was a week later, and Augusta, in her hospital bed, was speaking to Duke (still in his bathrobe) and to her visiting daughters. It was the first day she had been able to see anyone.

"The same red-haired man who saved me from drowning before. Remember Tennessee Valley? Remember how I kept seeing him?" She turned to the nurse and begged her, "Tell them."

"Very well, Mrs. Gray, but this is the last time, for you do tend to rave on about it, and that's not what's wanted for your healing." The nurse turned to Augusta's family. "She was brought into the emergency room in the arms of a young man, very tall. He was crying."

"He was crying!" Augusta interrupted excitedly. "Isn't that strange? Not aloud, mind you, but apparently tears were just streaming down his face. Streaming! And he was tall and red-haired, wasn't he?"

"Yes, Mrs. Gray, he was a redhead. And he called the hospital almost hourly for four days until he learned for sure that you were out of danger."

"And I've sent friends to look for him at his apartment, but he's gone and I don't know his name."

"But can't you tell the police anything about the person who shot you?" Duke asked. "All you talk about is this man."

"No. No, I remember nothing, nothing. I was thinking about my running trip as I left the hospital. Then I woke up in this room today, a week later! I've got to find him."

"No, dear, you've got to rest," said the nurse. "Everybody out now. Time's up."

Augusta almost died from the wound that had narrowly missed her heart. It was probably due to her fine physical condition and the strength of her heart that she didn't die.

San Francisco was in the grip of a series of "stranger murders" at this time—murders with no apparent connection between killer and victim—and her shooting was considered by the police to be one of these, although the press tried to make some connection between her husband's heart attack and her peripheral involvement in an automobile accident on Vallejo Street. She was much quoted. Everything she said tantalized the reporters and bewildered them. "Ever since I started running toward the writing of my International Jogging Book, cars have been trying to kill me, but not bullets. This was my first bullet since I started to run, although who knows how many people became enraged at the sight of my running and planned to gun me down? Besides my husband, I mean. I mean, he was not very pleased with my running. But he was bedridden at the time of the shot."

"You blame everything on your running book, then?"

"Oh, no. I blame no one and nothing. Money, of course, is always blameworthy, and marriage is the root of a lot of trouble, but running is pure happiness. But happiness can cause trouble—although I shouldn't think enough trouble to shoot someone about. Well, I *have* been running around looking awfully happy, and I think certain people do feel threatened by that."

"Do you think it was a stranger-murder attempt?"

"I guess it has to be."

"Who was the redheaded man who carried you into the hospital?"

"I don't know."

"Why was he crying?"

"I honestly can't imagine."

"Have you ever seen him before?"

"Yes, he saved me from drowning once."

It was all too strange, and the press loved it for about a week.

Augusta was a long time recovering from her wound. She waited for the red-haired man, but he never came. Duke left the hospital. Daniel left, but she remained. She got pneumonia. She couldn't quite recover enough to go home. Realizing that she could not go off on her trip right away made her lose heart. First she would have to get well, and then she would have to get back in shape. It all seemed beyond her powers. She would have to regain all her lost aerobics and powerful leg muscles. The very thought of running was wearying. She didn't want to go home. She loathed the thought. It seemed to her that everything was back to what it had been before, except that she was weaker and older and more scared.

She waited for the red-haired man to come and get her so that she would not have to go home.

Finally she did go home, still convalescent. The leaves dropped from the cherry tree. All anyone talked about was the drought. Val went off to Princeton, Lee into seventh grade. Duke got her to sign the traveler's checks so he could put the money in the bank. Most of it he reinvested in stocks, under his own name. She didn't care. Let him have it; it wasn't worth anything to her, and it was life or death to him.

Duke sold the Austin Healey, since she never left the house. She didn't care. He got her to sign the two remaining stocks—there was Princeton to pay for, after all—but he invested the money in real estate. In his own name. No matter. She realized she hadn't been intelligent about the money. He would build it up, and it would be there for the girls.

He plagued her and plagued her to find out about the missing twelve thousand, but she didn't tell him it was all in the pretty picture on the wall by her half-room bed, which was where she now slept. She would not sleep with Duke and did not pretend it was because of her convalescence. "I do not love you anymore," she said honestly.

"You could at least try. Aren't you willing to make an effort to put our marriage back together?"

"No, I'm not willing. I can't try. I don't want to."

"It's because you're still so frail. When you are feeling stronger, you'll feel differently."

"When I am feeling stronger, I will leave you," she said honestly. She always spoke honestly now. She was totally honest except about the Hiroshige. This was her only secret now, her only remaining deception, and therefore perhaps her only hope. It was the symbol of her dash for independence, her brief sprint for freedom. It reminded her of the days when she was a runner, her days of heightened perceptions, heightened senses, when the clear song of her self traveled for miles in the air. For whom do the reeds on the riverbank weep? For Augusta now.

Gradually she took up her housekeeping chores and prepared meals. Lee encouraged her to take up her running again, and she said that she would. She still nurtured a tiny, wavering flame of hope that the red-haired man would come for her, but she didn't talk about him anymore.

One day she went out the door and down the walk to the cherry tree. She looked at the quiet lane and knew she could go no farther. She was afraid. She had a monstrous attack of panic and fled back into the house.

"My agoraphobia has come back with a vengeance. I

talked to the doctor, and he said this is customary when someone has been violently injured on the streets and is a long time recovering. He says it is natural for me to be afraid. But I must try. Please help me."

Duke was too busy; nor did he see this as desirable. Val was away. There was only Lee who cared, and Augusta did not want to be a burden to Lee, did not want to be a "queer mother" for her, a mother whom she had to help and protect.

Her friends said, "Nonsense. Get hold of yourself, Augusta. You're all well now. This is silly. Granted it was a terrible experience for you, but it's over now. No one's out there waiting to shoot you. Come on."

But she was deathly afraid to leave her house. The world had shrunk down again, smaller than before her running. Before there had been her neighborhood, her town. Now there was only her house.

Now when Lee asked, "Aren't you still going to do the running book, Mom?" she was silent.

"I think you should. I'll help you. We can run together. It won't take you long to get good again."

"No, sweetheart. I just don't seem to care about it anymore."

Unless my savior comes, she thought. She dreamed of him coming for her, helping her, healing her as she had wanted to heal him, because only he understood her and cared for her.

She would tell herself not to indulge in this fantasy, that it was unhealthy, that she must help herself. But then she would remember how he had carried her to the hospital, weeping, and called hourly to inquire about her. She knew that he would come.

In late October—when all but a few leaves had fallen from the cherry tree and lay in desiccated heaps upon the lawn—he came to her door one morning.

They both looked shyly at each other and nodded, unsurprised. He looked different, younger; his face was open.

"You've come," she said. Tears of relief pricked her eyes. "I've been waiting for you."

Where had he heard that before? Ephraim wondered. Who had said those same words? Oh, yes. The man at Aikido of Tamalpais, where it all began. His father.

To Ephraim, Augusta looked older, ethereally pale. The light was gone from her face and hair. Her glow was gone.

"I've been away, doing a lot of thinking and writing, Augusta. I'm a writer, you see, and I've written a novel about you. And me. I'd like you to read it and give me your opinion."

"I'd be glad to. Now?"

"Can you come now? We will have to work together on it. There's a lot about your jogging book. You will want things added. We'll share the proceeds, of course. We'll be partners."

"I'll come. Yes, I'll come now—and may I stay? May I come and stay as your guest for awhile? I've been anxious to leave here but I've been unable to. Again I must rely on you to help me."

"Help you?" Ephraim was surprised. "Oh, well, of course . . ."

"Oh, thank God. You see, I've been waiting for you to come and get me. I'm all ready to go. Just one second . . ."

Augusta grabbed a sweater and took the Hiroshige from the wall. "Will you take the suitcase there? It's been packed for months. Since I last saw you—"she talked rapidly, overexcitedly— "or since you last saw me, that is. I don't remember you carrying me into the hospital. Not at all. But they told me. You saved my life. Again! And again you didn't let me thank you."

"Augusta, wait." Ephraim suddenly understood that she didn't know the whole truth. Somehow he imagined she had known but was protecting him. Should he tell her now? No, better to have her read about it in the book so that she could understand fully.

She was still talking. "I have been so afraid to leave the house, but now I can dare to go, with you beside me. And my picture will calm me. I will look at it the whole time until we get to your place."

"Has your agoraphobia returned?"

"Yes, I have been totally housebound, and as soon as I take one step out the door, I know I will be terrified." She appealed to him. "May I hold your hand?"

"Of course. But don't grip it so tightly. Relax." They walked out the door together. He buoyed her spirits as they walked to the car. "Just relax your mind and body. It's not the outdoors you fear or anything out here. It's your own fear that frightens you, the attack of panic you believe will overwhelm you. But it won't. It won't. I am beside you, and even if you faint, which you can't if you are relaxed, I will sustain you. Here we are."

They got into his Jaguar. She put the picture on her lap, and as they drove along, she imagined herself being poled down the river in the little boat, all washed by moonglow, with the soft, sweet sound of willow leaves susurrating in the night breeze.

In this way, she made a safe passage. Ephraim, sometimes glancing at the woman beside him, was moved by her, felt sorry and, also, felt happy at his response to her, at his fantastic new ability to respond.

Soon they were ensconced in his new apartment, which was very like the last. He left her undisturbed while she read his manuscript. It took several hours.

When she was done she praised him. "It's amazing. With so little to go on, it's an incredible work of the imagination that comes very near to the truth, in respect to me at any rate."

"Because it is true. It is almost all fact, Augusta, and some deduction."

"Oh, no. No, that's not possible. It can't be. . . . "

"Yes. You told me much of your life when we were together in the other apartment. I also had the tape. I have since talked to Daniel Swanson and Nancy O'Hara. The rest I was intimately involved in myself."

"But you . . . you . . . "

"I was an assassin. Was. I am not anymore."

"You mean you chose to cast yourself in the role of the assassin for the story?"

"Augusta, it is not a story," he said gently.

Augusta was quiet for a long time, absorbing this knowledge. "Not a story? All true? Even Quilp?" She fought it. "But you would *never* have shot me. You saved me. Twice you saved me. At the cove I know you saved me, because I was conscious. And at the hospital they told me that you brought me in and that you wept. Tears. Tears, Ephraim! That's proof."

He said nothing, waiting for her to credit this knowledge and handle it. She looked at him, saw that he would not speak, would not deny. She willed him to deny it. All she wanted in the whole world was for him to deny it. Otherwise there was nothing left for her. She would give up.

He remained silent.

"I . . . I see that you did shoot me. Yes, it's the only thing that makes sense of it all, isn't it?" she said sadly. "I had such a nice fantasy about you and me. Such a nice fantasy. It sustained me. It kept me going. Gave me hope. Now I have nothing. No one. But myself. And I am just a shadow. You missed my heart, but you got my spirit. Better you had got my heart."

"Augusta!" He made a gesture towards her, but she shrank from him.

"I must go now," she said. "I can't stay here with you." She turned and looked for her things. Slowly she put on her sweater, found her suitcase where he had put it in the bedroom. She got the Hiroshige from the mantlepiece where she had set it. Then she stood at the door, pale and trembling.

"Where will you go?" he asked.

"Home."

Ephraim turned his back to her and said definitely, "I will not take you back to Duke."

"You have to."

"I won't."

"But I can't go myself. I am too afraid." She began to weep. "This is so awful. It's so pathetic. Don't you think it's pathetic?"

"Yes." He came over to her and took the suitcase from her hand. "I'll leave you here alone. How's that? Perhaps if you think about what you've read, you will begin to understand and accept." He set the suitcase down.

"Accept that you shot me!" she bleated. "That you wanted to kill me! When all this time I thought you'd saved me!"

"So readjust your thinking. You can handle it. You're strong."

"I'm not at all strong." She grabbed up the suitcase.

"You don't mean that. You don't really want to be pathetic. Look, you believe in change, don't you? You changed. And I changed. Since the day I shot you I've been at a retreat, coming to terms with myself, writing this book. I'm done with killing. Believe me. Think about it. Think about us." He went to take the suitcase, but Augusta held on to it. There was a brief struggle.

"You and Governor Brown," she snorted.

"What?" Ephraim let go of the suitcase in surprise.

"I know these California retreats. Everyone goes and has a high old time. It's a big social event. All the best people are there. And they're always on the most beautiful property around, usually in some fabulous old mansion or ranch, since they're tax deductible. That's where you were while I was in a hospital bed trying not to die and when I was imprisoned at home trying to get started living again—all because of you trying to kill me."

Ephraim smiled. "Now you sound like your old self."

"You don't even know my old self."

"Yes, I do."

Augusta was getting weary of holding the suitcase, but she felt that to put it down now would be to give in. Give in to what?

"What did you mean by 'think about us'?" Did you say 'think about us' a minute ago?"

"Yes."

Augusta put down the suitcase. She was glad to put it down. "All right, I will."

"Good, I'll return in the morning, and we'll talk. We'll talk some more then." Suddenly he shut the door and was gone.

"Wait!" She ran to the door and called after him, "Ephraim!" But he had disappeared. She was all alone.

I won't panic, she thought. I'm strong. Ephraim said I was strong. Tough as nails I am. But what if he doesn't come back? What if I've lost him again?

She went to the telephone, put down the Hiroshige, dialed home, then picked up the picture again and held it close while she talked.

"Mom, where are you? I couldn't believe it when I came home and you were gone."

"I'm at a friend's."

"Who? Daddy called all your friends. He couldn't see how you got out."

Got out? It sounded so horrible that Augusta couldn't speak for a moment.

"Mom, are you there?"

"Yes, I'm here." She was silent again and then said, "I've left your father. I haven't left you, sweetheart, just him. I had to, you know."

"I know."

"Will you mind being with him for a little while until I figure things out?"

"No, not at all. Are you going to buy another sports car?"

Augusta laughed. "We'll see."

"You sound good, Mom. You sound better."

"Thank you, honey. I think, maybe, I'm going to be all right."

Augusta said good-bye and hung up. For a long while she stood there looking at the phone. Then she put the Hiroshige back on the mantle.

# 9

. . . . . *Not Waiting*

THE rising sun cleared a hill, and the yellow light of dawn splashed through the window of Ephraim's bedroom. Augusta woke from the best sleep she'd had in months.

The bedroom was pleasing. Ephraim had the secret of making a room look simple without looking bare. One wall was all books to the ceiling—an impressive library, including the books he had written under a pseudonym, books she remembered having read over the years. Now that she knew they were by Ephraim, it helped her to

*260. . .*

understand him, because she could compare the compassionless killer of the early books to the one in the manuscript.

She stretched and looked about. Yes, it was a nice room. She loved her little house, but it had become a prison. I would never have gotten well there, she thought. Not with Duke. I would have lived on in my little half-room, a half-life. Gradually I would have forgotten what it was like to be wholly alive.

She had meant to think everything through before going to bed, but she had fallen asleep immediately, like one stunned. Ephraim would soon arrive and expect her to have decided something about their immediate future.

She got up and put on the black velour robe she had bought for her travels. Gleaming on the lapel was a ceramic silver star that Lee had given her for a talisman. It was only slightly smaller than a sheriff's star.

She would need some coffee before she could think.

In the kitchen she was pleased to see that Ephraim liked a drip pot.

I will tell Ephraim that I understand about the killing, she thought as she put on the water and measured the coffee. It was his work. It was what he did for a living. I'll say, "I see that killing me was just a job"—she spoke aloud—"but I can't stay here with you. I want to work with you and be your friend, but"—she poured the water over the grounds—"I have a readjustment to make in my mind, such an enormous readjustment. It will take time. We must go slowly. And wait. Until . . . " What? Wait until when for what?

"Had we but world enough, and time/ This coyness, lady, were no crime."

No, Augusta, no quotes. You've got to do this on your own.

She poured the coffee and marshalled her thoughts. Every so often her lips moved.

Presently there was a knock at the door, and Ephraim entered.

"Good morning."

"Hello, Ephraim. Ephraim, I understand now . . . "

"Smells good. Is there more coffee?"

"Of course." She hastened to the stove and poured him a cup. Then she pulled her belt snug, clasped her hands, and began again. "I undertand that your killing me—your shooting me, I mean—was a job. You didn't want to kill me, but your career was at stake. You had to prove to yourself that you were still good, and if you could finish me off neatly, then the botch you'd made of the job could be forgotten. The botch," she repeated. She tried to recapture the thread. She looked at Ephraim, who appeared relaxed and attentive. He sipped at his coffee.

She spread her hands wide. "But how could you have missed such an easy shot? You, such an expert? I think there must have been an earth tremor. Don't you think there was a small quake, just enough to shake the ground a little and destroy your aim?"

He laughed. "You and your earthquakes. You're incredible. Don't you see it was a greater cataclysm than that? It was a soul quake."

"Because you had begun to feel?"

"Yes. Feel, not fail. I thought I was beginning to fail as an assassin. In fact I was beginning to succeed as a hu-

man. It will still take you awhile to understand that this
is not a story. It gives you pain to believe that I tried to
kill you, especially because you'd envisioned me as your
savior. But it's important for you to understand what I
was—a monster. And what I'm trying to become—a person. You mastered the art of living. You were the Angel
of Life, not I. I want to learn from you."

"Yes, I see. But I also see that you've saved me once
again. Yesterday you took me from prison, and I would
never have found the strength in myself to escape a second time."

Augusta dressed and they had breakfast together on his
small deck, which was lit by the morning sun and over-
looked the marsh where they both had used to run. Unusual clouds were building in the sky.

"Will you work with me on the book, then?" he asked.
"I can still sleep nights away if you wish, if it makes you
feel more comfortable. But I want to help you get back
into life. I want you to stay."

"I . . . I don't think I should stay here." She remembered she hadn't finished her speech. "I still have such
an enormous . . . " The words didn't seem to fit anymore. She sighed.

"Let's go for a walk."

"The thing is, Ephraim," she said as they went out the
door, "you don't really know me, nor I you. We just
have our fantasies of each other."

"True. But what powerful fantasies."

They walked a little way together on the marsh. The
day had become curiously dark. They discussed the
book. Augusta described her jogging routes and laughed

to tell of them. "I have them written down. I'll get them for you to add to the manuscript."

They walked along silently together, and as it began to rain, they turned back but did not increase their pace. Augusta was feeling so well, so relaxed. She wasn't experiencing any dizziness or distress. It was wonderful to be out of doors, to be with this extraordinary man whose presence seemed to have a magical effect on her. She felt that with him she would never have a boring second. She glanced at him. He looked beautiful in the rain, even more vivid. His hair was alight. What a flame of a man he was. She remembered running with him in Kapaolani.

Impulsively she stopped and turned to him. "Ephraim, I do want to stay with you, and I don't want you to spend the nights away. I want to be with you totally."

As she said this, she put her arms around his waist and hugged him. She felt his body stiffen. It was like embracing a tree. Surprised and concerned, she looked up at him. He smiled vulnerably.

"I'm scared," said the assassin.

"I'll be gentle," said the housewife.

## The End